WDM PRESENTS: SHORT FICTION FROM 2018

DEB LOGAN
DEBBIE MUMFORD

WDM
Publishing

INTRODUCTION

2018 was a very good year for WDM Publishing. We published several collections and relaunched a novel as well as releasing the short fiction included in this volume.

When they weren't working on future novels, our authors wrote short fantasy and science fiction tales, and even one spy academy story.

This volume opens with a sci-fi portal story, moves into the realms of fantasy, and then explores an exclusive academy that caters to spies. We end the volume with a Deb Logan middle grade science fiction story, followed by a moving space opera tale by Debbie Mumford.

We hope you enjoy the short fiction of 2018.

A WALK WITH GEORGIA

1

---

*W*ho knew that walking the dog could be perilous to my soul?

Georgia and I had just strolled around a curve in the duff covered path through a pine forest, when she stopped, gathered her haunches firmly beneath herself and prepared to attack. A low growl rumbled through her chest, filling the too quiet air.

I stopped by her side, puzzled. Georgia might be built like a tank — she's a very solid bull mastiff — but she's the gentlest, toasted-marshmallow gold giant in the dog world. She considers all children her playmates, and despite her size would happily climb into any willing adult's lap. And loyal ... words fail to describe the intensity of her devotion. Even on long walks through heavily wooded areas, she doesn't require a leash. She wouldn't dream of leaving my side, of leaving me unprotected.

Given her psychological make-up, this aggressive position deserved my attention. I didn't try to calm her. I scanned the trees for danger ... and immediately understood.

A visual anomaly hung in the air a few yards to our left. If Georgia hadn't reacted, I could have walked right past without noticing, but with my dog on alert the incongruity was impossible to overlook. The air shifted and trembled within a large oval that hung between two towering pines. Whatever it was, it wasn't connected to the earth, but floated a foot or two above the needle strewn forest floor. The edges wavered rhythmically, almost as though keeping time with a silent heartbeat, and while the center showed the grayed-out of a dusky woodland, the scene didn't match the forest where Georgia and I stood.

I could see huge lodgepole pines reaching for the sky behind the anomaly, but their massive trunks failed to bisect the throbbing oval that hung between me and them.

Time slowed. My pulse pounded, drowning out even Georgia's threatening growl. I wanted to reassure the dog, but words deserted me. Besides, my lips and throat were suddenly so dry I doubted I could even manage a croak. Primeval fear gripped my soul. The certain knowledge that death and the destruction of all I knew waited on the other side of an unknown that had suddenly become visible.

A shadow materialized in the center of the anomaly and my muscles unlocked. Adrenaline coursed through my veins; it was time to fight or fly, and I was no fighter.

"Georgia, come," I said, my voice harsh with fear. What if her instincts demanded that she fight? "Heel," I cried, and turned and ran.

She leapt forward with a threatening snap of her jaws, then turned obediently to chase me.

Too late.

I'd allowed my paralysis to last too long. I should've run when Georgia first brought the phenomenon to my attention. Our opportunity for escape had expired.

Wind whipped my hair as leaves and pine duff pelted my face. Saplings and undergrowth leaned precariously toward the strange oval. My leather jacket pulled me back as though some monster had grabbed me by its suede surface. I glanced behind me and saw that the shadow had become a vortex, the oval a dark maw, sucking my world into the unknown.

Georgia fought to stay beside me, the powerful claws I worked so hard to keep a reasonable length dug into the earth, creating furrows as she was inexorably drawn backwards. I grabbed a young pine, wrapping my arms around its trunk, gripping the rough bark with too soft fingers as my feet sought to lose contact with the ground. But what about Georgia? I couldn't let my dog be dragged into that maelstrom while I hugged a tree!

But what could I do? Even if I could reach her, my hold on her collar would be tenuous at best, and that single strap of leather about her neck might endanger her quite as much as the vortex that sought to pull us into who knew where. What if my attempts to save her snapped her neck? Why had I ever abandoned her harness and leash? With those I might have had a chance of tying her safely to a tree.

Her great brown eyes met mine and a piteous whine begged me to fix this. Me. Her source of food and shelter and love. Her world revolved around me. She looked to me with love and loyalty ... and lost her grip on our good solid earth.

"No!" I screamed as my faithful dog tumbled into that dark maw. Without a thought, I released the tree, my anchor to reality, and was sucked through the vortex which snapped shut behind me.

2

I woke to Georgia's warm breath wafting across my face. Thrilled though I might be to find we were both alive and together, her breath was ... doggy, in the extreme. Pushing her away from my face, I sat up, threw an arm across her broad back and surveyed our surroundings.

Her calm reinforced my own sense of no immediate threat. She sat quietly beside me, tongue lolling from the side of her mouth, ears forward, looking around with an air of serene contentment. I shook my head, amazed at the immediacy of a dog's life. She'd evidently put the horror of being dragged through a vortex behind her.

Too bad I couldn't do the same.

Clinging to my dog, the only familiar element in my current circumstance, I drew comfort from her nearness while trying not to infect her calm with my fear. Because I was terrified. I couldn't even say, "Where on earth am I?" because I was horrifyingly certain that the answer was, "Nowhere."

Wherever Georgia and I had landed, we weren't on earth. We sat in a small clearing surrounded by tall, well I don't know what they were, but they weren't trees, and whatever grew on the land around us, it wasn't grass. A deep purple creeper that might pass for some kind of succulent covered the ground, starred here and there with tiny white blossoms. The not-trees at the edge of the clearing were also colored in unearthly shades. Lilac roots and trunks blended into canopies of magenta, wine, and mauve.

Steeling myself, I raised my eyes to the sky. Instead of the cool blue scudded with fluffy white clouds of my home, I found a lemon yellow shell and two blazing discs, one a fiery orange, the second, and smaller, a juniper green so dark it bordered on black.

Suddenly feeling a deep kinship with Dorothy, I hugged my massive Toto and whispered, "We're not in Kansas anymore." Then I buried my face against Georgia's solid shoulder while I fought off the hysterical giggles that threatened to steal my breath, and very possibly my sanity.

When I felt a bit more in control, I straightened, accepted a loving swipe of Georgia's tongue, and stood, resting my hand on her head.

"Well," I said, "wherever we are, we're going to need food, water, and shelter, and I'm not at all sure we'll even recognize the first two if we find them." I glanced down at my dog. "I'm going to be relying on you, girl. Your instincts on what's edible or drinkable have got to be better than mine."

A happy "woof" answered me, and I stepped forward into an adventure I hadn't sought.

"On the bright side," I said aloud, more for my sake than Georgia's, "I'm dressed for walking and we'll get plenty of exercise." It had been a lovely fall day in the foothills of Colorado when Georgia and I left for our walk. She wore a red leather collar and I was dressed in layers. Jeans, warm socks and hiking boots covered my lower body, but my torso sported a black silk turtleneck, a dove grey T-shirt, and a green plaid flannel shirt, all topped by my chestnut brown suede bomber jacket. Except for a hat and gloves, I was in good shape for whatever weather this place might send our way.

We hiked through an unnatural stillness. No birds sang, no small creatures rustled through the undergrowth. Truth be told, there wasn't any undergrowth, just that deep purple succulent and the lilac not-trees. Georgia had marked the first not-tree we encountered when we stepped under the forest canopy. Evidently the odd colors didn't bother her. Of course, I wasn't really sure what she saw since humans and dogs perceive color so differently. But she was so nonchalant, I took a chance and ran my fingers over the not-tree's trunk.

I wasn't prepared for its silky smoothness, but I was even less prepared for its warmth, or the faint pulse I detected vibrating just below the surface.

Skin! Touching these not-trees was more like running my fingers over skin-covered flesh.

Jerking my hand away from what should have been rough bark, I urged Georgia forward. I suddenly felt less like a woman walking her dog through an oddly colored forest, and more like a small girl lost in a sea of strange men's legs.

The memory chilled me. I'd been about four, at church with my parents. Daddy had carried me into the vestibule after the service. He'd set me on my feet, instructing me to stand still while he helped Mother into her coat. I'd only wandered a few feet, but when I grabbed the pant leg of the man who stood beside me, I'd been startled to find a stranger's face looking down at me. The crowded room had suddenly seemed alien. All those legs clothed in dark suit pants, just like my dad's, but which of them was Daddy? I'd been on the brink of panic when Daddy's strong arms scooped me up and his wonderfully familiar voice said, "There you are! You're okay. Daddy's got you."

Remembered comfort flooded me, but departed just as quickly. I wasn't lost in a crowd of caring members of my church family; I was lost in an unknown place among who knew what these things that weren't trees were! If something leaned down and scooped me up, it wouldn't be into the arms of a loving father.

I picked up my pace, trying not to break into a panicked run —after all, I had no idea where I was going, but also trying not to allow so much as my jacket to graze any of the not-trees.

Gradually I calmed and began to take in the details of the not-tree forest. No undergrowth and the not-trees appeared to be very evenly spaced. Too evenly spaced. I stopped and turned a slow circle really looking at the rows of whatever they were around me. Rows. Evenly spaced. No undergrowth. These things ... these not-trees were being cultivated. Nothing grew wild with this kind of precision back home on earth, and I doubted that it did wherever the heck I was now.

Cultivation meant intelligent life.

Something farmed this land. And Georgia and I were trespassing.

3

---

*B*etween the excessive exercise — Georgia and I had probably walked further today than we normally did in a week — and the bursts of adrenaline that had pumped through my body, I was sorely in need of water. I knew Georgia had to be thirsty as well, so I gave her her head and hoped she'd lead us to water. Or something that passed for water and would be safe for canine and human consumption.

At long last we came to the end of the not-tree farm. Georgia paced slowly, head down, tongue hanging out. I stumbled after her, barely managing to stay on my feet.

"Just one more step," I'd promise myself. "You can rest after one more step." I'd one-more-stepped myself to the edge of exhaustion. I was on the verge of collapse, when Georgia's head came up and her ears perked forward.

Forcing myself onward, I followed as she picked up her pace and trotted almost happily to a small clearing. This one was covered in pale silver creepers with bright gold flowers. So many flowers that the center of the clearing appeared to be a pool of molten gold.

Georgia trotted straight to the center and buried her snout in the golden flowers. When she raised her head and looked at me, petals dropped to the ground like beads of purest honey.

She barked once and buried her muzzled back into the pool of flowers.

A pool of flowers? My nerves sizzled and dehydrated neurons flared. Water! Georgia had found water! I stumbled after her, falling to my hands and knees by her side. The silver creepers seemed to emanate from the pool, their golden flowers covered the surface, floating like interlocked water lilies.

Georgia had indeed dripped flower petals, having destroyed a section of the plants in her haste to reach the liquid beneath, but the liquid itself had a slightly yellow tint as I cupped it in my hands.

To drink or not to drink? I couldn't survive long without water. Die of dehydration or die of ingesting a poisonous substance? Neither sounded appealing. I glanced at Georgia. She looked fine. If the liquid was a poison, it wasn't fast-acting.

"Good dog, Georgia," I said. "You found us something to drink, and I said I'd trust your instincts. Here's hoping we've both made good decisions."

I brought my cupped hands to my lips and sipped.

I'd never tasted anything so good in my life. Cool. Thirst-quenching. Life-sustaining. The liquid had a light, sweet flavor, reminiscent of watermelon on a hot summer day. I sipped slowly, and then lay down beside Georgia to allow my body to accept what it had been given before I attempted another handful.

I closed my eyes and ran my tongue over dry lips, almost able to perceive my cells plumping, my energy rising.

Having drunk her fill, Georgia rolled onto her back and accepted my homage of grateful belly rubs.

The sky was darkening to a deep burgundy by the time I was satiated. We had no shelter, but having seen no living creatures other than ground cover and not-trees that day, I decided not to worry about it. I curled up next to Georgia and hoped that the temperature drop would not be too drastic. I fell asleep wishing I'd thought to bring water bottles, dried jerky, a sleeping bag and maybe a small tent on our walk that morning. But who expects to be sucked into a vortex to another planet, or plane of existence, or alternate universe when they head out to walk the dog for twenty minutes?

Adventure has never been my thing, and this one was certainly not planned.

4

Sometime in the middle of the night I woke to Georgia's deep-throated growl. With no moon or stars visible, I was as blind as if I'd had no eyes. I oriented on Georgia by the sound of her growls and rested my hands on her back. Her hackles were up.

A soft, sibilant whisper sounded in the darkness to my left, barely audible over Georgia's growls. My stomach fluttered and my pulse roared in my ears, but I stroked Georgia's back and managed to say, "Hush, girl. We need to hear." She quieted, momentarily.

Something poked my arm and I jumped.

Maybe something poked Georgia too. She lunged forward with a full throated bell. Her jaws snapped and I heard a horrible sound like tearing flesh.

More sibilant whisperings and shuffling like many small feet retreating.

"Georgia! To me!" But I needn't have called. My lap was suddenly full of heavy, warm dog, licking my hands and face, and whimpering. I held her tightly and wished fervently for a flashlight. Georgia rarely licked and almost never whimpered.

"Good girl," I whispered. "Brave, girl." Whether I was praising Georgia or admonishing myself, I'll never be sure. Sleep banished, I waited for a new day to dawn.

Morning revealed a small dusky green carcass. The creature had a squarish body with no discernable head, six appendages, three of which had multiple stick-like fingers. Georgia had torn one appendage off and mustard-yellow blood oozed from the damaged areas.

I assumed it was dead. It didn't move and I had no way of guessing as to its vital functions. I could vividly imagine one of those stick-like fingers poking me in the utterly lightless night.

"What do we do now, girl?" I asked Georgia. "We killed one of them, and we have no idea how many more there are, or even where they are." I pondered what I knew so far, which was abysmally little. "Do they not need light? Do they only come out at night? Are they the farmers, or just a small nocturnal species?"

I drank my fill, and considered whether or not the creature might be edible. But since Georgia had not gone near the body after killing it, I decided the odds were against that particular food source.

Cursing my lack of a container, I reluctantly left the pool. Surely we'd find another before our need was too great. Before we took off, I encouraged Georgia to sniff the remains.

"Find more, Georgia," I encouraged. "Find a settlement. We aren't going to find our way home alone, so we might as well look for more of these creatures."

She's not a hunting dog, but she's smart and she seemed to understand what I wanted.

We soon left the silver creeper behind and moved onto a plain of waist-high tubular plants. Deep plum color. Like leafless bamboo. If this plain had been planted, it had been sown by broadcasting the seed rather than planting in organized rows.

With no watch, no working smartphone, and no familiarity with this sky, I had no way to tell time, but we hadn't been walking long before Georgia's ear's perked up and her pace moved from slow plod to interested trot. I had just noticed a dark area on the plain when Georgia disappeared into it.

With a cry of alarm I hurried forward to discover that she had trotted down a gentle slope into a circular depression. From the rim, I watched as she moved to the center, circled once staring into what might have been entrances around the perimeter, and then settled to the ground and looked up at me, head cocked as if to say, "Why are you still up there?"

I sighed and made my way down the slope to join her. Whatever happened, we were a team.

I crouched down beside her and patted her head. "Good, girl. What have you found?" At regular intervals around the edge of the depression were what might have been entrances to fox dens or rabbit warrens. "Did you find a community?" I asked. "Are we right in the middle of the town square?"

She wagged her tail and sneezed.

"Well, if anyone wants to meet us," I said, sitting down. "They'll have to come out. I'm not crawling down a rabbit hole, and you don't look like you're exactly itching to explore either."

We sat quietly. Georgia rested her head on her front paws and closed her eyes. I leaned against her side, stroking her head or scratching behind her ears. After what seemed like eons, but was probably less than an hour, Georgia's ears perked forward and her eyes opened. No other movement signaled her change in alertness. I peered around, trying not to move my head, but anxious to detect what she'd heard.

I felt it before I saw or heard it.

A small tickle in the back of my brain. Not the back of my neck. Nothing touched me physically. No. I felt that tickle *inside* my skull.

My heart slammed against my ribs, my lungs seized. Terror clawed at my mind.

But Georgia remained calm. No raised hackles. No deep-throated growls. Just my dog, resting by my side, with her ears perked forward.

I'm not in physical danger, I told myself. *Georgia would know if I were being threatened.*

I breathed in deeply, forcing myself to calm.

Then I felt it again. More distinctly. Like a scratch inside my skull.

What? I thought. *What is it?*

Us, came the answer.

My hand stilled on Georgia's back. I closed my eyes and concentrated on my senses. On the feel of Georgia's fur beneath my fingers, the barest whisper of a breeze across my cheeks, the odd, sweet / salty / fecund smell of the plum-colored bamboo, the dryness of my mouth, and the emptiness of my stomach. I catalogued each sense and then moved past them into a part of my mind I'd never used. There I sensed a barely there thread of energy. A filament of thought not my own. I touched it.

And light blazed through my soul.

I saw them, the denizens of this world. Not a dead carcass that I couldn't tell what the pieces parts might be, but intelligent beings who understood their universe far better than I understood mine.

We communed. A true hive mind, they had no individual names or identities. Each organism functioned as the whole directed. They shared their world with me and drew out my understanding of my own. They called themselves Craylons.

They were curious about Georgia, what she was, her relationship to me, why they'd been unable to establish contact with her. Ahh. She was other than me. Not yet evolved, but cherished none the less.

Their mind was vast; their knowledge so much more than my single brain could comprehend. Even so, I understood. The Craylons only emerged after both suns had set. The combined radiation from the pair created a deadly peril for them. They had not developed eyes since they were never exposed to light.

But eyes or not, they were an inquisitive species, always seeking to increase their knowledge. Georgia and I had been pulled from our world during an experiment in one of their scientific facilities.

Forgive us, they said. *We did not intend you harm.*

I understand, I replied. *Forgive us as well. We were frightened. Georgia is a gentle dog and would never have killed except to protect me.*

The death of one is mourned, they said, *but the many continue. We will study the experiment and find a way to return you. Will you be content to wait?*

I smiled and hugged Georgia. What choice did we have? *Of course,* I replied. *We appreciate your hospitality.*

Darkness fell, but it held no terror. Creatures moved around us, but I held Georgia steady. Food and drink appeared and the light in my mind guided my fingers without the necessity of sight. Georgia and I ate and drank and slept in peace.

It might not be tomorrow, or even next week, but Georgia and I were going home. With all the Craylon knowledge my single human brain could carry.

COPYRIGHT

TO HAVE...AND TO HOLD

PROLOGUE

*M*y name is Artie Woodward, and I'm the happiest girl alive.

Wow! I never thought that phrase would apply to me, especially when I was a kid. I mean, I'm a seer. I see things normal people don't, things they couldn't see, even if they wanted to, which no one in their right mind would. I mean, even I don't want to see the terrors, but I don't have a choice. I was born with this strange ability to see the unseen, to know the unknowable.

I thought I was alone. Thought I'd spend my whole life alone.

Sure, my mom and dad loved me, but even they thought I was weird. They worried about me constantly and dragged me to more shrinks than I care to remember. None of them helped. After all, they all thought I was imagining things. Except I wasn't. So I learned to hide.

I became adept at hiding. I hid my knowledge from my parents. I tried desperately to hide my weirdness from the kids at school. But most importantly, I hid the fact that I could see them, that I knew they existed, from the terrors themselves. And as long as I hid, I stayed safe.

Lonely, but safe.

So how did I grow up to be the happiest girl in the world? How did my life change from hidden and lonely to fulfilled and glowing with contentment?

Jed Kendrick found me.

We recognized each other, and our loneliness ended. We were both seers, and on our first day at McKinley High we became a team, but that's another story. Suffice it to say we've fought terrors together for nearly six years and have developed an unshakable bond.

And along the way, we fell in love.

And now, I'm the happiest girl in the world because in late September I'll become Jed Kendrick's wife, and he'll become Artie Woodward's husband. The Woodward-Kendrick team will be official in the eyes of the world.

But first, we had to make a pilgrimage to Ireland. Jed's grannie insisted.

1
——————

On a beautiful summer day in mid-August, Grannie O'Toole met us at the Dublin airport. We emerged from a sea of people to find her waiting for us, an island of calm in the form of a small, lean woman with frizzy gray hair that Jed assured me had once been curly and deep red.

"Jedidiah Kendrick," she called, opening her arms and stepping toward us with lively impatience. "Come and give your grannie a hug!"

Jed obeyed without hesitation, wrapping the little woman in his long arms and lifting her right off the airport's tiled floor.

"It's so good to see you, Grannie," he said as he placed her gently back on her feet. He grinned like a loon as he released her and angled his body to include me in their conversation. "Grannie, this is Artie, the love of my life." His eyes twinkled as he reached for my hand. "Artie, this is Grannie O'Toole, the best Irish grannie a boy could ever dream of."

Grannie O'Toole reached for my other hand while still maintaining a firm grasp on my husband-to-be. As our fingers met, a circle of energy clicked into place. Suddenly, the three of us really were an island in a sea of people. The pervasive buzz of voices around us muffled, people flowed past us without seeming to notice our existence. We were a rock in the stream that they avoided without awareness.

Grannie nodded. "I wondered," she said, her voice calm and quiet. "I knew Jeremiah was a seer from the moment of his birth." She turned her faded hazel eyes on Jed. "You held the potential, but Jerry held the power. Even here in Ireland, I felt the change when he died and you accepted the mantle."

Jed startled. I felt the slight pull of his fingers on mine, saw his gaze tighten and focus as he stared at his grandmother. "You knew?" he asked. The question held a tinge of accusation, and I heard his unvoiced thought. *You knew what I was and you didn't bother to explain? Left me to discover everything for myself?*

"Aye, child. I knew."

Jed tried to withdraw, to pull away from this woman he thought he'd known, but she held him. She must've been stronger than she looked, for my big, strong man failed to break the continuity of our circle.

"Be at peace, my boy," she said in that calm, quiet voice. "It's part of the curse of our blood that we cannot acknowledge one another until our power is fully developed. I could no more help you to find your way than you'll be able to help the next seer in our line." She turned her attention to me. "But you," she said, "you're a surprise. I wondered about the young woman our Jed had fallen for, worried that she might be Fae. 'Tis why I insisted on meeting before the wedding. If you were less than human, I needed to ensure you revealed your true nature before my boy took vows that would bind him to you for eternity."

I was the one who startled now. Every instinct I owned urged me to hide, as I'd done so effectively before Jed and I found each other, but I willed myself to stillness and looked Grannie O'Toole straight in the eye. She met my gaze without flinching and I read nothing but sincerity and warmth.

"Fae?" I asked. "As in fairies? Are fairies real then?"

Her eyes widened. "Of course they are," she exclaimed. "Are you telling me you've attained the years necessary to contemplate marriage without ever encountering the Fae?"

My jaw dropped and I turned my gaze on Jed. "Is she saying that the terrors are really fairies?" I asked. "I always thought fairies were little winged creatures who danced in mushroom circles and slept on flower petals."

Grannie guffawed, there was no other word for the snort of laughter than emanated from her small body, pulling my attention back to her.

"Sorry," she said. "I can see we've a lot of catching up to do. Let's break this circle and speak of normal things until I get you home. My house is warded, strongly warded, against the Fae. We won't need physical contact there in order to have a private conversation."

And so saying, she broke our contact, as easily as if we'd both been toddlers. While she'd been able to hold me like a vise, I had no more luck clutching her fingers than I would've had capturing a moonbeam. I had the feeling Grannie O'Toole had a lot to teach me.

Thank all that is holy, I was absolutely correct.

2

———

*G*rannie O'Toole's house was a charming cottage in the Dublin suburb of Shankill. With its whitewashed walls, jewel-red front door, overhanging thatch roof, and blue window boxes filled to overflowing with red chrysanthemums and white baby's breath, the cottage was everything I'd ever imagined of finding in Ireland. The only thing missing from my perfect vision was its setting. Instead of being surrounded by acres of rolling hills in brilliant shades of emerald green, the little cottage was hemmed in on two sides by neighboring homes and in front by a heavily trafficked cobblestone street.

The three of us piled out of the cab Grannie had hired at the airport and soon stood with our meager baggage — a backpack and duffle for Jed and a carry-on size rolling case for me — in the street in front of Grannie's cottage. As we approached that red door, I felt a slight resistance, as if the house pushed me back to the street. An overwhelming urge to walk past swept over me. I stopped, glanced around, and noted a puzzled expression on Jed's face. He felt it too.

Grannie smiled, placed one hand on the door, then held her

other out to us. "Touch my hand," she encouraged. "Just a finger will do."

When both of us complied, she nodded and said, "Jedidiah Kendrick and Artemis Woodward are welcome in my home. Please, come in."

The resistance vanished, as did my need to walk away.

Of course. Grannie had mentioned that her home was warded against the Fae. Evidently those wards worked against seer blood as well, and Jed and I had now been invited inside their protective shield. I shivered, but held my questions until we were safely inside those innocent looking whitewashed walls.

"I wasn't sure if you'd want to share a room," Grannie said breezily as she led us into a comfortable, lived-in front room. A well-worn sofa upholstered in a tweed fabric the green of budding leaves and heaped with throw pillows in bright jewel tones rested before an authentic fireplace complete with stone hearth and a planed log mantle. Two overstuffed chairs in matching upholstery provided additional seating. "But seeing as you're only handfast and not actually married, I've given you each your own space." She grinned. "That, and I didn't want to give up my own room!"

She led us through a cheery kitchen with white pine cabinets and pretty lace curtains, and up a narrow staircase. I hadn't expected a second floor and found myself on a compact landing between two doors leading to identical small rooms tucked under the cottage's eaves.

"These were originally children's quarters," she explained as Jed and I separated and stowed our luggage in the windowless cells. Each was furnished with a single twin bed covered with a colorful quilt, an old-fashioned washstand complete with basin and ewer, and a drawer unit cunningly built into space beneath the eaves. The sloping roof meant Jed could barely stand in his room, and only near the door. "They're tight, but you'll not be spending much time in them."

We trooped back down the stairs and Grannie completed the tour with a glimpse of her bedroom, spacious and sunny compared to the upstairs rooms, and a shared bath complete with old-fashioned claw-footed tub.

At her insistence, Jed and I settled in the front room while she bustled around the kitchen making tea. Once we were all possessed of steaming cups with a rose patterned plate of short-bread cookies resting on the pine coffee table, Grannie returned to the subject of seers and fairies.

"So," she said, settling into the depths of her overstuffed chair. "Tell me about your experience of the Fae. What did you call them? Terrors?"

I glanced at Jed, waited for him to take the lead.

"That's what Artie named them," he said with a nod in my direction. "She's seen them since birth. Like you said in the airport, I didn't see them until Jerry died. He was the seer, I was just his twin."

Grannie turned to me, her blue eyes seeming to pierce my very soul. "I know Jed's bloodline," she said, "know he inherited his ability from my line, but what about you, young woman? How do you come to see the Fae?"

Grannie's scrutiny unnerved me. Without thinking, I angled my head so that my long dark hair shadowed my face, closed my eyes, and concentrated on hiding, on being invisible. Stillness settled over the room and as I counted my heartbeats, I calmed.

Until Jed placed a hand on my arm.

"It's okay, Artie," he said, his tone soothing and soft. The kind of voice he'd use with a startled horse or a frightened child. "You're safe here. Grannie's no threat. She's family. No need to hide."

I opened my eyes and straightened, grasping Jed's hand and

meeting his gaze. I nodded. "You're right," I said and turned my attention back to Grannie. "I'm sorry. You startled me and I reacted without thinking."

She stared at me a moment longer, then said with a sigh, "You've a powerful defense, Artie. Almost I lost sight of you ... and me a seer. I could feel the power coalescing around you, cloaking you, and even so I nearly lost the knowledge of you."

She glanced around the room, and following her gaze I glimpsed pale runes shimmering above windows and doors and centered on walls before they winked out of sight.

"If it weren't for my wards, I think you'd have succeeded in disappearing from my mind completely." She shuddered and took a sip of tea from the rose patterned cup she still held. After a moment, she continued. "Well, I think we've established you've seer blood. From a very potent bloodline. An ancient bloodline."

"More ancient than ours?" Jed asked.

She nodded. "I've never known a seer with that kind of power, but there are legends..." Another pause while she sipped more tea. I could almost see the thoughts tumbling through her mind as she considered.

"Legends?" Jed prompted when the pause grew lengthy.

"What?" Grannie startled, her eyes widening, as though she'd forgotten our presence. "Oh. Yes. Legends. Among the Fae, there's a legend of a pair who will defend the human race, who will banish the Fae to another realm. Make it impossible for them to feed off our fears and baser instincts. A pair who will free us from them for eternity."

She studied us over the rim of her cup. "I wonder..."

I frowned. "That can't be us. I mean, if we were destined for something, wouldn't someone know? Wouldn't *we* know? And how do you know about Fae legends anyway?"

"It's my family's," she gestured at Jed with the cookie she'd just plucked from the plate, "*our* family's business to know.

We've spied on the Fae for years, kept journals of all we've learned. Journals I'll be handing on to you now, my boy. Now that I've seen for myself that you've the sight and your intended is the right sort as well."

Biting into the shortbread cookie, she chewed, swallowed, and took another sip of tea. "The best thing the Fae could do, if they felt the time of the legend approaching, would be to isolate the families. If your parents, and therefore you," she pointed at me with the half-eaten treat, "were isolated from those of us who know and understand what the Fae are, you'd come into your power without benefit of training. Without understanding our ancient enemy. You'd be weak, and easily destroyed."

"As Jerry was," said Jed, a stricken look marring his features.

"Exactly," Grannie said. "Except for an accident of birth, Artie's partner would've been destroyed and she would've gone to her grave without ever reaching her potential, discovering her destiny."

"But because Jed and Jerry were twins," I said, catching the direction of Grannie's thought, "Jed's potential awakened when Jerry died." I squeezed his hand tightly. "And fate brought us together."

Jed gripped my hand with both of his and gazed into my eyes. "Not fate," he said. "Divine intervention. Don't forget Michael. Don't discount Dad's dream that sent us to Colorado."

"Michael?" Grannie's voice was so sharp I felt like she'd pounced on the name with a tiger's unsheathed claws. "Who is Michael?"

Releasing my hand, Jed leaned forward, elbows on knees, and gazed directly into Grannie's eyes. "Michael, the hunter. The archangel. The commander of God's armies. At least, that's who I've always known him as."

Grannie's eyes narrowed. "And how exactly do you know this Michael?"

"I first saw him when Jerry lay dying. When my sight awoke. Everything changed, and when I looked around, I not only saw the thing that had killed Jerry, but I saw him ... the angel ... Michael, standing behind my father, his eyes full of sorrow and pity. That's actually the only time I've ever seen him when I was awake. Every other time he's come to me in dreams."

"In dreams?" Grannie prompted.

"Yeah. He's used dreams to teach me. To tell me how to fight the monsters, the terrors, as Artie calls them. He's given me strategy and curses or spells to defeat them. I'm pretty sure he's the one who visited Dad in the dream that caused him to move us across the country to Artie's hometown. He knew she needed me. That we needed each other."

She nodded, crossing herself quickly. "An angel. Well, imagine that. And here I thought I'd be the one training you." Dusting the shortbread crumbs from her fingers, she stood, collected our tea cups and turned toward the kitchen. "The pair of you really are special if an archangel has chosen to involve himself." She paused, and glanced back over her shoulder. "Since you've little formal knowledge of the Fae, we'll start your education bright and early in the morning."

3

The next few days were full of wonder. Who'd have guessed that I'd have to go all the way to Ireland to read fairy tales? Of course, these particular tales were true.

Grannie pulled out the family journals and we spent every evening studying the Fae. Jed and I learned about the various races of Fae, about their courts and their powers. We learned the places they were most likely to be found, the hills and rings and raths that covered the British Isles and much of Europe, places Grannie felt sure were portals to that other dimension where their true home lay.

We also learned about ley lines. Lines of power which connected those sites, running in straight lines from point to point and which the Fae traveled in processions ... invisible to all but those with seer blood. If an oblivious human had the misfortune to build a structure across one of those lines, death and destruction followed when the next procession occurred.

During the days, Grannie O'Toole took us to church yards and ruins and circles of standing stones, whatever we'd studied the night before. On one such outing we visited a construction site. All three of us could clearly see the blue ley line shim-

mering with energy in the morning sun ... and running diago-
nally through the steel bones of what would someday be an
upscale shopping mall on the outskirts of Dublin.

Grannie sighed and shook her head. "'Tis a shame it'll never
be completed. The Fae travel this path every year at Samhain.
Halloween," she added, correctly interpreting my confused
expression. "I tried to warn the owner, but he laughed in my
face. Fairy tales are for children, and the gullible, don't you
know?"

I shivered, glad I'd be safely home in Colorado long before
Halloween came around. The terrors I'd learned to battle at Jed's
side were bad enough, but here, in the Old Country, the number
and variety of Fae were daunting.

Everywhere we went, we saw Fae. Some were kindly, child-
sized brownies caring for domestic animals or lending an
unseen hand with household chores; some were tricksters,
dwarves and goblins amusing themselves by moving keys or
hiding reading glasses; but others rivaled the terrors in their
malicious intent, feeding on their victims' positive emotions so
that the individuals were left with only distrust and sociopathic
thoughts.

Grannie O'Toole cautioned us to act as though we were
oblivious to the presence of the Fae, no matter their type.

"Don't see them," she advised. "Whatever you do, never look
directly at a Fae. If you must observe them, do so only with side-
long glances or have a reason to look past them. Focus on a bit of
the landscape beyond where they stand."

Jed bristled at this advice. "Artie and I don't ignore them. We
fight and banish them."

"Maybe at home you can afford to fight," she said with sad
resignation. "Colorado must be a wonderful place if there are so
few Fae that two young people can fight and win. But not here.
Not in their stronghold. There are too many, Jed. You and Artie

would be overrun and destroyed — or worse, taken as their playthings — in a heartbeat."

"If we are the legendary pair," Jed argued, "how are we supposed to defend the human race and banish the Fae by pretending we're not what we are?"

Grannie poked a finger in his chest, her expression fierce. "You'll defend our people by lying low until you know enough to fight. Remember Jerry. Remember what happens when a seer tries to do that which he's not yet strong enough to accomplish!"

"That's not fair," Jed said through clenched jaws. His voice was low and controlled, but I heard the anger simmering just beneath the words. "Jerry was a child. I'm an adult."

"Jerry was untrained," she retorted, "and you've only just discovered the existence of the Fae. You didn't even know enough to know what you were battling back home in Colorado."

I stepped between them, placing a hand on Jed's arm. "Enough. You're fighting over how and when to fight."

Grannie stepped back, and Jed turned his gaze on me.

"I don't like letting them get away with things," he said, quietly, but with a sullen edge. "They're hurting people."

"I know," I said, stroking my hand down his arm until I could entwine my fingers with his, "I don't like it much either, but I think Grannie's right. We need to hide our knowledge until we've learned all we can here … and then we need to plan."

He nodded, some of the fire leaving his eyes. "You're right. Whether or not we're the pair in their legend, we won't do anyone any good if we take on more than we can handle right now."

Grannie sighed loudly, but held her peace.

"Let's take a break," I suggested. "We've only got two more days in Ireland. Let's do something fun. Grannie," I said, turning to include her in the conversation again, "there must be something we can do that has a low probability of running into the Fae. What do you suggest?"

Grannie's brow furrowed slightly, then cleared as she nodded and smiled. "That's a grand idea, Artie, but I'm thinking we should take it a step further. Why don't we take a break from each other as well as the learning? I've some errands I've been avoiding, and I'll be surprised if the pair of you wouldn't like a bit of time together without me hanging on your every word."

I opened my mouth to protest, but the twinkle in her eye combined with the happy surprise on Jed's face kept me quiet.

She laughed with delight. "As to where you should go, you might enjoy the Dublin Zoo or the National Botanical Gardens. Both are tourist attractions and full of people, and therefore Fae, but if you wander the less traveled paths, you should be safe enough from their notice."

"That sounds lovely," I agreed.

Jed stepped to Grannie and drew her into a hug. "I'm sorry for picking a fight with you," he said, kissing the top of her frizzy head. "You're right, of course, and an afternoon of sight-seeing will give me a chance to clear my head."

She leaned back and reaching up, patted his cheek. "You're a good boy, Jedidiah Kendrick, and I'm pleased and proud to be your grannie."

Stepping out of his embrace, she swiped tears from her eyes with the back of a hand before using it to make shooing motions at us. "Be gone with you now. You can catch a bus to either the zoo or the gardens at the pub where we had dinner last night. Have a grand time and I'll see you this evening."

Unfortunately, we decided not to catch a bus from the pub in Shankill.

4

_____

I'd just come downstairs from gathering my purse and a light jacket when Jed caught me in his arms.

"Alone at last," he whispered in my ear, and then his lips found mine.

My whole body responded to his kiss. My pulse skyrocketed while butterflies played tag in my belly; my toes even tingled. I was warm and happy and ... home. It didn't matter that we were in Ireland, if Jed and I were together, I was home. They say that "home is where the heart is" ... and Jed was, and always will be, my heart.

We broke the kiss, and I laid my cheek against his chest, listening to the steady beat of his heart. My arms encircled his waist, and his held me close, resting his chin on the top of my head.

"I've missed this," he said. "Time together, just the two of us."

I nodded, rubbing my cheek against the soft cotton of his favorite moss green shirt. "I've enjoyed meeting Grannie," I said quietly, "and I've learned so much, but I'm glad we're going home soon." I straightened, leaning back in his arms to smile up at him. "We've got a wedding to plan!"

He grinned back at me. "We certainly do." A slight crease in his brow signaled a change in subject. "Listen, do you mind if we don't go the tourist route? I'm not in the mood to be squashed on a bus and then mingle with hordes of people."

"Fine by me," I said, stepping out of his arms and catching his hand in mine. "We can see zoo animals and flowers back home."

"Good. Let's just take a walk instead. There's a really cool ruin just through the woods. Mom took Jerry and me there once. I think we were about six during that visit," he mused. "Every other time we saw Grannie, she came to us. Lots more affordable to fly one person across the Atlantic than four ... or even three."

A shiver skittered down my spine, but I associated it with the mention of Jed's dead twin, not with intuition. I wish I'd heeded my subconscious mind's subtle warning.

"That sounds perfect," I said instead. "It's a gorgeous day for a walk."

Jed led me down the street, around the corner, and into a children's play park. On the other side of the manicured lawn, an old growth forest brooded. Grabbing my hand, Jed strode quickly toward the trees. As we approached, an opening in the undergrowth appeared and I saw a path of dark earth strewn with moldering leaf duff.

We stepped under the trees and the village and all its modern sights and sounds faded away. A world of shadowy greens and browns enveloped us; no sound reached our ears but a low breeze moaning through the leafy canopy.

I squeezed Jed's hand, reassured by the warmth of his fingers. He grinned down at me.

"Don't worry," he said, pulling me forward into the forest, "this is nothing. The castle is even spookier."

"Wow," I said. "Way to reassure a girl." I rolled my eyes, but laughed at myself and picked up my pace. No need to make the man feel like he was dragging me to my doom.

The day was warm and the woods were still. I felt a bit like I was walking through a dream. To dispel that illusion, and just for the comfort of hearing his voice, I asked, "So where are we going?"

"There's this really frosty ruin in a meadow just the other side of these woods. It's called Puck's Castle. Jerry and I thought it was great when we were kids."

Sunlight glimmered through the canopy, and I realized we'd reached the edge of the woods. Just beyond the trees lay a paved road with the forest lining one side and a low rock wall on the other. We crossed to a metal gate and I had my first sight of the ruin.

Puck's castle looked like a giant's face, mouth open in horror, eyes slitted against a wind only it could feel. A cap of green hair trailed across one corner of its brow.

I shivered. "Why is it called Puck's Castle?"

Jed glanced from the stacked rock ruin to me. "You know, I hadn't thought about that, but I remember now," his brow creased in a frown. "It's supposed to be haunted by a pookah, a mischievous fairy who plays the pipes and hops around on the rocks."

That was when I noticed the muted glow of the ley line.

I grabbed Jed's hand, tugging him back toward the cover of the trees. "We have to go, Jed," I said, trying desperately to mask the hysteria rising in my chest. "Now. We have to go NOW!"

The glow of the ley line was no longer muted. The iridescent blue brightened as I watched, pulsing as though to a musical beat.

Jed ignored my panicked tug. He stared across the meadow to the forest on the far side of the castle.

"Jed," I cried. "Please!"

If he heard me, or felt me yanking on his hand, he gave no sign. My love, the man I intended to marry, stood as though turned to stone and stared as a troop of fairies left the shelter of the woods and marched along the ley line straight to Puck's Castle.

Too late, I thought. *Leaving now will only draw their attention to us.* So I did what I had always done, I hid in plain sight. And prayed that my gift would shield Jed as well.

I peered through the curtain of my dark hair, watching the approaching fairies through slitted eyes. One of their number peeled off and scampered up the rock tower, lithe as a mountain goat. When he reached the top, he danced from stone to stone, lightly skipping over the ivy that trailed in a glistening stream across one corner. His dance ended abruptly on our side of the castle, and I knew I'd been unsuccessful. The pookah saw us ... or at least one of us.

His surprised cry caused the troop to halt, and me to close my eyes and redouble my effort to hide.

But my attempt was in vain.

Footsteps pattered across the green carpeted meadow, and I cracked my eyes open by the merest sliver to see the pookah and two tall, silver-haired companions standing on the other side of the gate from us.

Jed shook his hand loose from mine, as if I were no more than a bothersome fly, and stepped toward the fairies.

"Begone," he said. "You're not wanted here."

"How unusual," said the pookah. "This mortal has eyes that see."

"Unusual and unacceptable," said one of his silver-haired friends. The creature crooked a finger at Jed and said, "Come, mortal. You must meet our queen."

My Jed, my partner, the love of my life, placed a booted foot on the lowest rail of the gate and began to climb over, his eyes glazed, his expression vacant.

I couldn't stand still. I couldn't let them take my Jed!

Flinging my invisibility away, I grabbed Jed's arm. "Jedidiah Kendrick, hear me! Come away, Jed. Come away with me now!"

The three fairies startled, stepping back a pace.

"What's this?" cried the pookah. "From whence did this mortal appear?"

"She holds great power," said the second.

"No matter," said the third, the one who had held silent until now. He turned gleaming orange eyes on me and spoke directly to my soul. "Come. Your will is mine. Follow where I lead."

I barely had time to duck my chin and close my eyes before his words wove their spell. A nearly irresistible urge to climb the gate and follow Jed into the meadow flooded my heart and soul. But a sliver of my will had managed to hide, and that sliver fought the fairy's compulsion. If I fell under his spell, who would rescue Jed?

The thought of losing myself wasn't nearly as terrifying as the thought of losing Jed.

That sliver of self blazed with fear for my love, and the hot emotion broke the fairy's hold on my mind. I slipped into my own spell and the creatures forgot my existence. Jed was their one and only prey.

When the troop had passed, I sank to the ground and sobbed, grieving for the life we'd never share now. I'd been powerless to protect Jed, and my heart ached with loss.

*G*rannie was inconsolable. She paced the floor in front of the hearth and wailed her despair, while I held myself together, folded into one of the overstuffed chairs.

"He watched them cross the field? He stood there bold as brass and stared at a procession of fairies?" Her eyes were red with weeping and her voice scratched and cracked as though she'd inhaled a lifetime's cigarette smoke. "Did he learn nothing from me?"

She pulled her already frizzy hair, and then turned on me. "And you ... how did you come home again, lassie? How are you here and not my Jedidiah?"

My own tears were gone, washed away in the flood I'd shed on the lane outside Puck's Castle. I had nothing left to give.

"I hid," I said. "I tried to shield him too, but they saw him anyway."

"You hid," she said, the words dripping scorn. "You claim to love my boy, but you did naught to save him. You hid."

"I tried," I answered, stung by the injustice of her accusation. "I cast away my protection and tried to call him back. He loves me. I love him." I sighed, futility washing over me yet again. "I thought my call would be stronger than theirs. I was wrong."

"Then how are you here?"

"I realized it wasn't working," I explained. "My sudden appearance startled them, gave me just enough time to slip back into my trance." I closed my eyes and rested my head in my hands. "Even so, I almost didn't make it. The only thing that saved me was the knowledge that Jed was lost if I gave in."

Her hand settled on my hair and stroked; the touch comforted me.

"I'm sorry, Artie," she whispered. "This is none of your doing and 'tis wrong of me to lay blame at your feet."

I rose and hugged her tightly. "I'm so sorry," I whispered. "I don't know what to do."

We separated, staring at each other through bleak eyes.

"How do we get him back?"

Grannie closed her eyes and sank onto the sofa, pulling me down beside her. "Oh, child," she said. "He's lost and there's nothing we can do about it."

I bristled, hot anger replacing despair. "I can't accept that," I said. "I won't accept that. I need him. We need each other. There has to be a way to steal him back."

She patted my arm. "I've never heard of the Fae releasing one of their toys," she said, but something in my expression made her change tack. "We'll search the old texts. Not just our family journals, but those in the clan library."

"Is yours the only seer clan?"

Grannie pursed her lips and thought. "I know a few other families. I'll ask them to search their journals as well."

I nodded, suddenly too weary to hold up my head. Research. It wasn't much, but it was hope, and I would cling to hope until I could cling to Jed again.

"Go to bed, Artie," Grannie said with a pat on my knee. "Neither of us is thinking clearly at the moment. We'll start our search in the morning."

I nodded and found my way to the second floor, where I was now the only occupant.

6

Our search was long and arduous, but Grannie O'Toole was a steadfast guide. We read every word of her family journals before moving to the headquarters of her ancestral clan, the O'Connors, and petitioning to search their library.

Fortunately, the O'Connor library was located in Dublin. Unfortunately, the older texts were indecipherable to me, and eventually proved beyond Grannie's skill at translation as well.

Days dragged by, followed by plodding weeks of reading ancient script until my eyes ached. Family and friends in Colorado called asking when Jed and I were coming home. I prevaricated, misled, and outright lied. I couldn't bear to tell anyone that he'd been stolen, kidnapped by supernatural creatures. No one would believe me anyway, so I hid behind a façade of a holiday too delightful to bring to a close.

August's myriad greens turned to the golds and reds of September with no solution in sight. Despair seized me by the throat as our anticipated wedding date approached ... and passed with me no nearer to rescuing Jed. I couldn't go on like this. I couldn't live without him, but I couldn't give up while he might be saved. Maybe the next document would hold the secret. I kept searching

By mid-October we had reached the limits of our ability to research, and I was desperately afraid I'd be forced to leave Ireland ... to abandon the possibility of ever seeing my love again.

Just when our spirits had reached their lowest ebb, Laird Angus O'Connor sought us out. He found us in a dim library chamber where tattered scrolls and decaying journals lined shelves set against stone walls dark with age. An ancient oak table occupied the center of the room, its wood so stained and dark it seemed to absorb what little light filtered through the high, narrow windows. The most ancient scrolls dealing with the Fae resided in this room ... scrolls filled with script that had defied even Grannie's ability to read.

The clan leader was an impressive man, with a broad chest, heavily muscled arms, a thick neck, and a full head of deep auburn hair. Though he was clean shaven and wearing a perfectly tailored suit, he looked like a warrior of legend.

"Maeve O'Toole," he called in a booming voice that filled the narrow chamber. "I've heard tales that you and your young assistant have fair taken up residence among the journals of our clan. Do you seek specific knowledge, or are you merely broadening your understanding of your heritage?"

Grannie scrambled to stand, so I followed suit, but when she gave the man a low bow, I merely inclined my head. He was not my laird, nor was he ever likely to become so, the way our search was going.

"Laird," said Grannie, standing as tall as her slight frame would allow. "We're looking for specific information ... regarding the Fae."

"I see." He shot a piercing look at me, and I saw wariness and a shrewd intelligence in his gaze. "And who might your assistant be? If she's of our clan, I've no recollection of her."

Grannie folded her hands in front of her and lowered her gaze. "She is not of our clan ... yet. Laird Angus O'Connor, may I present Artemis Woodward. Artie, this is my clan leader, Angus O'Connor."

Laird Angus held out a massive hand, and I laid mine in it.

"'Tis pleased I am to make your acquaintance, Miss Woodward," he said, lifting my hand and brushing my knuckles with his lips. As he did so, a flash of recognition seared my mind. This man was not only a seer, he was far older than his looks suggested.

He smiled, a twinkle lighting his eyes. "Ah, I see your blood recognizes mine. Good. That will expedite matters." He released my hand, sat down at the long narrow table between the racks of books and scrolls, and gestured us to chairs as well. "What do you seek, and how may I assist you?"

Grannie raised an eyebrow in my direction, but remained silent. I sighed. I preferred to leave the explaining to her, but obviously she'd decided this was my tale to tell.

"Very well," I said, and gave my full attention to the laird of the O'Connors. "I'm engaged to Mrs. O'Toole's grandson, Jedidiah Kendrick. We came to Ireland so that Grannie could meet me before we married. Once here, we discovered that Grannie is a seer, like Jed and myself. However, we found Grannie to be much more knowledgeable, so we set out to learn what we could from her before we returned home to the United States, to our home in Colorado."

I told Laird Angus everything I could, every detail of how Jed had been taken and how I'd escaped. The telling was hard. During the weeks Grannie and I had searched for answers, I'd tried not to think about that day, tried not to remember exactly how I'd failed Jed. Instead, I'd concentrated on finding a solution. But it had all been in vain.

Grannie and I avoided speaking of the future. I lived in her house and we worked side by side searching the records for clues, but I knew in my heart I couldn't stay in Ireland forever. Yet, I couldn't imagine returning to Colorado without Jed. Frankly, I couldn't imagine living without Jed. If I left the Old Country without him, what point would there be for my existence?

And so I stayed, would continue to stay, until I found Jed or Grannie sent me away.

As I finished my tale, Laird Angus took my hands in his and stroked them with his thumbs. Compassion filled his gaze as he said, "Ah, lassie, 'tis sorry I am to hear of your woes, but the chances of you regaining your love are very slim."

Tears filled my eyes, but I blinked them back. "I know," I whispered. "Actually, they're about gone since even Grannie can't decipher these final journals."

"I can see you're a steadfast lass," he said, releasing my hands, "but have you courage as well as loyalty?"

I swiped at my eyes to clear the tears and met his gaze. "I've dealt with terror since my earliest memories, and did it on my own until Jed found me. We were in our teens by then. Together he and I fought the terrors, the Fae ... and won. Until we came here." I lowered my eyes and studied the delicate opal ring Jed had given me when we agreed to marry. "There are so many more Fae here, and we had so very much to learn. I guess we failed."

Laird Angus lifted my chin with his index finger until my eyes met his. "I may know a way," he said, "but you'll have to act alone, and it will require more courage than most seers possess. I'll not fault you if you choose to leave this place with the tale untold."

My heart leaped. My pulse thundered so hard I could barely hear past its whooshing against my eardrums. "Y... you ... you know how get Jed back? Tell me," I demanded. "Tell me now!"

"Oh, Laird!" Grannie said, and she looked so white I worried she might faint.

The big man laughed. "Call me Angus," he said. "We've no need for formalities between us. We're seers all, with much work to be done."

The plan was simple to tell, yet seemed impossible to execute.

As Angus explained, all I had to do was pull Jed out of line as the fairy troop processed along a ley line during a full moon ... and hold him until he recognized me.

"You can see them, so you can do it," Angus assured me.

"It sounds too easy," I said, frowning. "What's the catch?"

His eyes darted around the room as he looked for something to focus on that wasn't me. "The catch, as you say, is that you must hold him no matter what the fairies do. No matter what spell they throw at you." He sighed and met my gaze. "Their own laws dictate that they cannot harm you during the rescue attempt, but if you despair, if you lose hold of him for even an instant, both of you will be lost beyond recovery."

"Beyond recovery?" Grannie said, and I heard the fear and tension in her voice. "What does that even mean?"

"Exactly what it says, Maeve," Angus answered. "Only one attempt is permitted for Jed, and since Artie will be attempting to steal from the Fae, no attempts will be tolerated on her behalf. Either they both come home, or neither does."

I nodded, then made eye contact with each in turn. "That suits me fine. If I can't save Jed, I've no reason to go on."

Angus nodded, a fierce glare in his eyes. Grannie's eyes brimmed with tears, but she bit her lip and made no objection.

7

---

*H*alloween, or Samhain as the Celts called it, brought the next full moon.

Grannie and Angus prepared for the attempted rescue by creating a shield bracelet for me and embedding it with every protective sigil and ward they could discover. Angus also took my engagement ring and sealed it with a spell to enhance the love it represented.

"We can't go with you," he explained, "can't help you with this task, but we can see to it you carry as much positive energy with you as is physically possible."

I spent my preparation time writing down everything I could remember of the time Jed and I had spent together. From our first meeting in social studies on our first day of high school, through every battle with every terror we'd ever vanquished, right down to the way he'd kissed me before we walked to Puck's Castle on that fateful day. Those memories strengthened me. They reminded me of all we'd accomplished, of all we'd become to one another.

Jed was my life and I was his. No matter what, I would hold him. Nothing a fairy or a terror or any other foul thing that walked our earth could do would cause me to abandon my man. Jed was the other half of my soul and I refused to continue to be separated from him.

Halloween morning dawned clear and bright and biting with cold. The time had come. Tonight the moon would be full and the fairy troop that had stolen Jed would process right through the middle of an under-construction mall on the outskirts of Dublin ... the one Grannie had shown us early in our visit.

"You're sure it's the same troop?" I asked, wiping damp palms on my well-worn denim jeans. "If he's not there, we'll have to wait for the next full moon."

"I'm certain, Artie," Angus said. "I've had spies out for the last few weeks. Experienced seers who know how to watch without being caught. Jed is with this troop, and except for being completely enthralled, he is whole and well."

I nodded, busying my fingers with binding my long dark hair in a single tight braid. I'd have no need to hide behind my hair this night. "Good. That's good."

"Come, Artie," Grannie called from the kitchen. "Let me fix you a nice dinner. You'll need your strength tonight."

I shook my head, remembered she couldn't see through walls, and called back, "No thank you, Grannie. I'm too nervous to eat. Besides, I'm stronger than I look. I'll be fine."

She hurried in to the front room a few minutes later carrying a tray of steaming mugs. "I thought that might be your attitude," she said with a wan smile. "Here, at least drink this broth. It'll fortify you without weighing you down."

"Good thinking, Maeve," Angus said with an approving nod, accepting his own mug. "Drink up, Artie. It'll be time to leave before you know it."

Angus and Grannie drove me to the construction site, timing it so we arrived just as the moon rose full and bright above the horizon. Grannie hugged me and wished me well, while Angus touched my ring and bracelet. "You're well warded, lassie, and ye've a stout heart. I've no doubt ye'll prevail."

I nodded and spoke past the lump in my throat. "We'll see you soon. Both of us." I licked lips that felt more like sandpaper than flesh. "But, if anything goes wrong, you have our story. Add it to your journal, please."

"There'll be no need, at least not until you've added another fifty years' worth of tales."

A quick grin and I left them to hide myself behind a pallet of bricks that was stacked beside the shining ley line. All that remained to be done was to wait for my love, my life, my Jed.

The moon floated just above the horizon, so round and full it seemed to fill the sky. A shining white orb starred with mars and craters against a velvet black sky studded with pinpricks of light. Surely such beauty boded well for Jed's rescue.

A soft jingle of bells wafted across the silent night. They were coming.

I hunkered low in a sprinter's crouch, one eye on the ley line, ready to spring the moment I saw him. My pulse raced, my vision wavered, my ears rang with nerves.

The first fairy appeared. An ageless female in a flowing green gown holding aloft a branch of silver leaves threaded with tiny golden bells. Behind her came a tall raven-haired male garbed all in deep blue carrying a purple banner trimmed in golden threads. Next came a throng of fair folk, easily thirty or forty individuals of all species, including a few Grannie hadn't described. Another bannerman and bell-bearer brought up the rear.

He wasn't there! Jed wasn't part of the procession!

How could we have been so wrong? What could I do now?

I closed my eyes against a suffocating wave of despair. And

then I heard the clip-clop of horses' hooves on the moon-drenched ground.

My eyes flew open and I beheld a snow white unicorn following the final bell-bearer. The ethereal creature had appeared as if out of thin air, and sitting sideways upon his back was the most beautiful lady I could ever have imagined. The female was dressed in gossamer fabrics, like moonbeams on an icy lake, in shimmering shades of palest blue, rose-petal pink and tender green. Her face and form were perfectly proportioned, an alabaster complexion framed emerald green eyes and her hair had the shade and shine of molten gold.

Surely this must be the fairy queen the pookah had spoken of, I couldn't imagine her as anything else.

My heart leapt and my soul stilled almost before I realized what I had seen. Jed walked beside the queen's horse, his hand resting lightly on her slipper clad foot, his eyes glazed and unaware.

My moment had arrived.

I sprinted from my hiding place, knocking Jedidiah to the ground. Encircling his left wrist with my right hand, I threw my left arm around his neck and clung to him like a burr.

Jed spoke not a word, but lay like a mannequin on the ground beneath me. Could it be this easy? Could I have won already?

Almost I loosened my grip, but the ring on my left hand and bracelet on my right flared to life and I felt their protective sigils glow.

No, I hadn't won. I'd merely surprised my enemy. The battle had yet to be engaged.

The fairy queen called out in ringing tones more beautiful than I could describe. The troop stopped. All eyes focused on me ... and Jed.

Unpronounceable, unknowable words tumbled from the queen's lips ... and my reality transformed.

I no longer held Jed. Instead I clung to the head of a giant snake that raised itself ... and me ... into the sky. I closed my eyes and chanted a mantra to the man I knew I held though the evidence of my senses told me otherwise. "You are Jedidiah Kendrick and I am Artemis Woodward. I love you and you love me. Come back to me, Jed!"

The weaving head faltered, the massive jaw closed, and a huge forked tongue darted out, tasting my scent upon the air between us.

The fairy queen spoke again, commandment in every unknown syllable.

The snake shifted and I no longer clung to smooth scales. Now my left arm wrapped the coarsely furred neck of a Bengal tiger, while my right hand fought to hold its claws from my flesh. Golden eyes stared at the pulse in my naked throat and knife-sharp teeth gleamed in its open mouth.

I closed my eyes and held on still more tightly. No matter what form the fairy queen forced upon him, I refused to release my Jed. If she made him kill me, so be it. I'd rather die than fail him again.

Fear clogged my throat, but I opened my eyes, stared straight into his, and screamed, "You are Jedidiah Kendrick and I am Artemis Woodward. I love you and you love me. Come back to me, Jed!"

The tiger's claws relaxed and something flickered behind his eyes.

The fairy queen spoke again, her words strident and somehow desperate.

Jed writhed and bucked beneath my hands, but I refused to release him. When the transformation was complete, I found myself eye to eye with the biggest bird I'd ever seen. My left arm encircled his neck, pulling a razor sharp beak too close to my face, while my right hand held tight to the pinion of his left wing.

Intelligence flashed behind his eyes as he cocked his great head and blinked a nictitating membrane. I smiled, with more courage than I felt, and repeated, for the third time, "You are Jedidiah Kendrick and I am Artemis Woodward. I love you and you love me. Come back to me, Jed!"

He lowered his feathered head, touching my forehead with his own.

"I love you, Jed Kendrick," I whispered, "and I will never let you go."

The fairy queen spoke again, but this time her voice held defeat. The great bird that had been Jed deflated and morphed and became ... Jedidiah Kendrick, a mortal man with his two feet planted firmly on the ground.

Jed stared into my eyes from where we stood, my right hand in his left, my left arm flung around his neck. He raised his right hand and caught the tear sliding down my cheek on his index finger. "I see you, Artemis Woodward. I know you. You are the love of my life."

Neither of us even glanced up when the fairy queen spoke. We had eyes only for each other.

"Congratulations, mortal female," she said, her voice distant and cool. "By the terms of our law you have won back my thrall. He is free from this troop, but I warn you, do not linger on these shores for all of my other troops will be anxious to avenge this slight. I now know both of your names and I do *not* wish you well."

Jed and I held each other without speaking until the troop had disappeared and Grannie and Angus ran to embrace us.

EPILOGUE

*T*hanksgiving is a uniquely American holiday and Jed and I celebrated it in Colorado with our families ... by pledging our lives to each other. Since our ordeal in Ireland had given us so much to be thankful for, we decided Thanksgiving was the perfect day for our wedding.

Grannie O'Toole arrived the day before, accompanied by Angus O'Connor. Jed was honored beyond words that the head of the O'Connor clan would come all the way to America just to attend our wedding.

I'd explained how Angus had been instrumental in Jed's rescue, but my love remained vague about the weeks of his captivity. Everything I told him of that time seemed to slip from his mind as soon as I said it, but I didn't mind. In fact, I envied him his forgetfulness. If I could erase the memory of my despair and grief, I'd do it gladly, except that it would also erase my knowledge of Grannie's steadfast support and how hard Angus had worked to help me bring Jed home.

The ceremony itself was a small affair. Jed and I exchanged our vows in the little neighborhood park where we'd first become a team. I wore a clean-lined white velvet dress, full length and long-sleeved in deference to the late November chill, and carried a small bouquet of gold asters and wine-red chrysanthemums. Jed looked regal in a black tux and a cummerbund, the latter in a deep gold shade that matched his aster boutonniere. Reverend Kendrick, Jed's father, officiated, and our vows were witnessed by Jed's mother, my parents, and Grannie and Angus.

Reverend Kendrick's face fairly glowed as he recited the age-old words, "Jedidiah Amos Kendrick, do you take Artemis Lucia Woodward to be your wedded wife, to love, protect, and cherish, to have and to hold from this day until the end of time?"

A slow smile spread across Jed's face, lighting his eyes and making him even more handsome than usual. He squeezed my hands. "I certainly do."

His father turned his gaze on me. "And do you, Artemis Lucia Woodward, take Jedidiah Amos Kendrick to be your wedded husband, to love, protect, and cherish, to have and to hold from this day until the end of time?"

The memory of those moments when the fairy queen had transformed my love from one deadly form to the next flitted through my mind. I had held him then, I would hold him forever.

"I do," I said without a single doubt.

Jed pulled me into his embrace and our lips met in a kiss that caused everything around us to fade into the background. I'm sure his father intoned the final words of the ceremony, but I didn't hear them. I didn't need to.

I was Jed's and he was mine ... and there wasn't a terror or a fairy in sight.

What could be more perfect?

COPYRIGHT

TO HAVE...AND TO HOLD

Copyright © 2018 by Debbie Mumford
Published by WDM Publishing
Cover and Layout copyright © 2018 by WDM Publishing
Cover design by WDM Publishing
Cover art copyright © Whiteisthecolor | Dreamstime.com

FAERY BEAUTIFUL

PROLOGUE

*F*amily holidays are the best. Especially this year. Now that I know I'm a faery, destined to live out my exceedingly long life in the Faery Realm, I'm careful to enjoy my human family. While I have them.

Take today. I don't think I've ever fully appreciated how nice it is to celebrate Thanksgiving with family and friends. Even though she's a few months into an unexpected pregnancy, Mom decided to go all out this year. She invited my best friend Lexie's family—Lexie, her parents Mr. and Mrs. Davis, her twin brothers Nick and Doug, and her baby sister Candy—Brent Rodgers, Lexie's boyfriend and my confidant, and, of course, Roddy, my erstwhile dragon guardian and current faery prince of a boyfriend.

The day was wonderful! The house smelled of roast turkey, apple cider, cinnamon, and fresh baked apple pie. The twins raced around causing mayhem, and Candy toddled into everything, with Mom beaming at them all.

"I've forgotten what it's like to have little ones in the house," I heard her whisper to Dad. "Next year we'll have a new addition to be thankful for."

Dad pulled her into his arms, placed a hand over her tummy and said, "We have a lot to be thankful for this year."

I turned away, smiling. It's great to see your parents so obviously in love. Even if the baby they're expecting is a consolation prize from the King of Faery. My many-times-removed grandfather had expected to steal me away when Roddy presented me to the Faery Court at Halloween. Grandpa had expected me to arrive in Faery and never leave, so he'd used magic to ensure Mom conceived while the parental units were sunning in the south of France. He'd also expected to execute Roddy for his supposed crimes. Needless to say, things hadn't worked out exactly as Grandpa had planned. He hadn't expected me to be so, well, me!

But everything worked out well. Roddy was not only alive, but his curse had been lifted and he was now back to his true form, a faery prince instead of a dragon. Mom and Dad were happily expecting a new addition to the family, and I was the acknowledged heir to the throne of Faery ... while still attending Jefferson High and living at home with my parents.

And best of all? Grandpa allowed me to tell Mom and Dad and Lexie and Brent all about being a faery princess and having magic. He placed a geis on them, of course. They're only allowed to speak of Faery with others who already know my secret, but at least I no longer needed to lie to my family or my best friends.

Life was good.

I sighed contentedly and sipped my hot chocolate. The feast was over and everyone had gone home. Well, everyone but Roddy. My prince sat beside me on the worn dark leather sofa in our family room, one arm draped around my shoulders, his feet propped on the sturdy walnut coffee table.

"I'm very fond of this room," he said, gazing at the braided rug in front of the fire. One of the burning logs popped, sending a shower of sparks up the chimney. "I spent many happy evenings curled before that fire, watching you covertly, and listening to you and Deirdre talk."

I rested my head on his shoulder. "Gran and I both loved you as a dragon," I said, remembering the great golden beast he'd been when we first met, "but I'm so glad Grandpa lifted his curse." I snuggled a bit closer, and his arm tightened around my shoulders. "I love you even more in this form."

"He only released me because of you," he sighed. "He'd fully intended to have me executed."

"I know," I whispered. "I remember."

I took another sip of chocolate, then leaned forward and placed my mug on the coffee table. While I was sitting forward, out of his embrace, I turned to look at him.

"You've never told me how Grandpa came to curse you in the first place," I said, frowning slightly. "I mean, I know it was all tied up with his daughter marrying a mortal, but I've never understood why he blamed you for her choice."

Roddy sighed, pulled his feet off the coffee table and onto the floor, and sat forward with his elbows on his knees. "It's a long, sad story," he said. "Are you sure you want to hear it?"

I nodded and, scooting to the corner of the sofa to give him some space, curled up to listen. "Tell me the story of Princess Rhiannon and Eoin the Strong. I want to know how my family came to be and why I'm now a faery."

1

Rhiannon was my best friend. She and Blodwen and I did everything together. All of Faery rejoiced in our friendship, the High King's daughter, the heir to Winter, and a daughter of Summer. What tragedy could befall a kingdom where all three courts were so inextricably twined?

Granted, Liannan, the Summer Queen, would've preferred to have her son and heir, Prince Idris, in our ranks rather than Blodwen, but Idris was young and Rhiannon and Blodwen and I were of an age.

From the time we were in the nursery, the three of us were inseparable whenever the three courts came together for celebrations. As we grew, we found ways to play together even when we were in our separate demesnes. Magic is a wonderful aid to mischief ... especially for royal children. After all, who but our parents could deny us?

Besides, who would want to separate us?

All of Faery was enchanted by our friendship. A young prince who was growing into a handsome young man, and two princesses, each more fair than any other lass in the kingdom. Rhiannon with hair as dark and midnight, eyes the color of emeralds, and the pink of spring roses in her cheeks. Blodwen, with her golden hair, violet eyes, and creamy complexion, was Rhiannon's best friend and confidant and her equal in every way.

I think many in Faery expected me to wed Rhiannon. They hoped she and I would ascend the throne of the High King, and my younger brother, Bran, would rule the Winter Court. But Rhiannon and Blodwen and I laughed at their expectations. As beautiful as the princesses were, I wasn't interested in either of them in a romantic way. Not even when we reached marriage-able age. They were my best friends, as close as sisters. I loved them both, but not as potential mates.

And that's when our idyllic existence began to fall apart.

When King Alberic realized that Rhiannon and I were not inclined to marry, he began to search elsewhere for a suitable mate for his only daughter ... without consulting her.

And in so doing, he planted the seed of our mutual destruction.

2

---

*R*hiannon's faery steed raced along the enchanted river that divided Faery from the mortal realm. She glanced over her shoulder and urged the stallion to greater speed with hands and heels. She knew I would catch her if she allowed her pace to slacken. My charger, heavier boned than Rhiannon's mount, couldn't match her mare's speed, but the charger's depth of chest meant he could maintain his pace far longer.

Rhiannon, stop this nonsense. I sent my thought winging to her mind.

She bent lower over her mount's neck and replied in kind. *It's my life, Rhydderich Drest Guerthenmach. I won't be auctioned like a prize heifer.*

You are a princess of Faery, I countered, layering my mind-voice with soothing overtones. *You've known all your life this day would come, especially once we made it clear that* we *didn't wish to marry.*

Her misery bled through our mind-link and I fought to stay calm, to keep from empathizing with the tears I felt stinging her eyes. Her will faltered, and the mare slowed her pace. I had won. Rhiannon acknowledged my argument.

My princess had been raised with every comfort: beautiful clothes, rich foods, precious jewels, faery folk to entertain or obey her slightest wish. Every indulgence had been granted my dear friend. Everything but the desire of her heart. More than anything, Rhiannon craved her father's love. The King of Faery had ensured his only child possessed every physical trinket a girl growing to womanhood could need or desire, but he had denied her his love.

King Alberic had loved Rhiannon's mother fiercely — and that love had killed her. Queen Morgana died giving Rhiannon life. Alberic never forgave the child for murdering his wife, or himself for desiring the heir that had cost him his love.

As I drew even with her, Rhiannon dashed the tears from her cheeks.

"Forgive me, Roddy. My tantrum has winded your charger."

"Gobhniu always needs exercise, my princess," I said, slapping the horse's neck as we slowed to a walk. "I only feared Danu might miss a step and break one of her dainty legs."

Rhiannon ran her fingers through Danu's golden mane. "You needn't have worried. She's far too sure-footed for that."

I bowed my head. "As her mistress is far too level-headed to flee to the mortal realm to escape her father's will."

A crimson blush suffused her face, but she held her head high. "It is my right. Every faery maiden is allowed a visit to the mortal realm before she weds."

"Yes, but not every faery maiden is the sole heir to the throne of Faery. You are unique among us, my princess."

"Still, I claim my right. Will you accompany me, Roddy? I cannot compel you."

I straightened in my saddle. "You have never needed to compel me," I said with dignity. "Even if your father had not charged me with your safety, you and Blodwen are my dearest friends. I would follow you to the end of the world."

Rhiannon smiled through her tears. "Thank you, Roddy. You are a true friend."

We urged Danu and Gobhniu to an easy canter and headed for the door in the rock that led to the land of men. I studied Rhiannon as we rode. She'd grown to womanhood in my company. We'd played together as young children and she had cheered me on when I entered the training lists at ten. I'd been knighted at fifteen, years earlier than was usual, but none of us, not Rhiannon nor Blodwen nor I, had ever been content with the usual. Once knighted, my princess had requested me as her guard. After all, if she had to have a faery knight following her every footstep, she'd prefer that knight be a trusted friend.

King Alberic agreed. After all, nothing in Faery threatened his daughter, the guard was merely a formality. A left-over tradition from a time when the faery people warred with the race of men. I think Alberic hoped that continued close association would lead us to declare our love and petition for permission to marry. A marriage between the High Court and Winter would save him the tedious process of marrying her off to a foreign prince, though if he had to arrange such a marriage, he would ensure it produced a profitable alliance.

I controlled my charger with practiced skill. The enormous horse responded to the slightest movement of hand or heel. I knew Rhiannon admired the man I'd become. She often teased me that I was strong of arm and lean of leg, epitomizing all a prince of Faery should be. But I knew her teasing was good-natured. Her way of letting me know she recognized my quality even if she didn't want to marry me.

She and Blodwen both found me handsome, commenting on my high forehead, strong chin, long straight nose, and deep green eyes. Rhiannon especially liked my thick golden hair, often plaiting it when we were young. Now my hair was clubbed at the base of my neck, not flying in the wind as did her waist-length midnight curls.

A shimmer in the air announced our approach to the enchanted portal.

I reined in Gobhniu and patted his neck. "Are you certain you want to do this, my princess?"

Rhiannon's gaze flitted to the magical doorway.

Beyond that threshold lay the realm of men. Neither of us had ever seen a mortal man, but we imagined them to be uncivilized brutes, incapable of wit or compassion. And yet, faery maids clung to their ancient right to dally with the sons of man. There had to be something attractive about the mortal creatures. Why else would our immortal maidens insist on such a tradition?

"The king has decreed my marriage to the prince of the wood elves across the Eastern Sea. Once I am wed, I will lose my ability to cross the threshold. It's now or never, Roddy."

"Aye, it is, but you did not answer my question, Rhia. Do you *want* to cross the threshold, or are you simply baiting your sire?"

Her cheeks flamed again and she shook her heavy mane of hair, but her defiance melted when she met my gaze. She sighed. "You know me too well, my friend. I'm angry with father, it's true. No matter what I do, he refuses to see me as anything more than chattel to turn to his profit."

She swallowed and turned her attention to the shimmering gate. "He's never loved me, Roddy, and now he's auctioned me off to the highest bidder, for an alliance we don't even need." She straightened in her saddle and gazed squarely into my eyes. "I intend to experience the other world before I lock myself in yet another loveless cage."

I bowed my head and placed a hand over my heart. "I wish I

could change your destiny, Rhia, but since I cannot, I will protect you from misadventure."

Rhiannon smiled, straightened in her saddle, and urged Danu toward the gate. "Do we take the horses, or step through on foot?"

"Afoot, I think," I answered. "I've heard our horses aren't fond of their mortal counterparts."

She nodded, flipped her heavily embroidered skirt aside and dismounted in a fluid motion. I joined her before the gate and we stepped over the threshold in perfect unison.

A cyclone met our booted feet, enveloped us in warm wildness, and separated us. I glimpsed Rhiannon's green skirt swirling around her slender body, her dark curls whipping upward in a mass of tangles, before the whirling madness forced me to close my eyes. The wind supported us into the mortal realm, but when I opened my eyes again, I found that it had deposited Rhiannon on a flat rock in the midst of gray-blue water, while I was dropped on an island ... in front of the shimmering portal door.

"Rhia! Are you all right?"

She grinned and called back, "I'm fine, but why am I here and you there?"

"The whim of magic?" I asked with a shrug. "Be still, my princess, I'll see if there's a boat on the other side of the island." I clambered over the rocks and around the curve of the island, losing sight of my princess, my friend.

3

"*B*e still, indeed," Rhiannon muttered as Roddy moved out of sight. "What else would I do on a rock in the middle of a lake!"

She pulled a comb from her pocket, sat down, and using the still water for a mirror attacked the snarls in her thick black hair. She'd nearly tamed the knots the cyclone had left in its wake when a prickle of unease raised the tiny hairs on the back of her neck and arms. Tucking the comb in her pocket, she glanced warily toward the shore. An enormous red-haired man stood watching her through narrowed eyes. He held the reins of a powerful roan horse while the animal drank of the lake's clear water.

So this was a human man. An unbleached linen shirt covered broad shoulders, while a red and green plaid kilt displayed strong legs and feet clad in supple leather boots. A huge sword hung in a scabbard at his waist and a hunting bow showed above his shoulder. Bright copper hair was clubbed at the back of his neck.

Rhiannon shivered at the intensity of his gaze, but remembered her station and rose to her feet, holding his gaze all the while.

"Why do you stare, mortal? Have you never seen a maiden before?"

"I've never seen beauty such as yours," he said, his baritone voice rich with admiration. "You astound me, lady."

And he astounded Rhiannon. His voice and words defied her expectations. A shiver ran down her spine and she wished faeries could swim.

"How came you to be on that rock, my lady? Do you require assistance?"

Silence enveloped her. What could she say? *A magical whirlwind deposited me here and I have no boat?* She smiled.

He leapt to his saddle with more grace than she had imagined possible for such a large human and urged his horse into the water.

Rhiannon's pulse pounded. What could she do? Precisely nothing. The rock offered no hiding place and no space to run.

The horse lost his footing, but the big man soothed him and urged him forward. The steed swam to Rhiannon's rock.

Before her addled mind thought to scream for Roddy, the man scooped Rhiannon from her perch and turned the horse back to shore. She clung to him like a burr on a saddle blanket until the horse stepped onto dry land. Once out of the water, she pushed his arms away and jumped to ground, whirling to stare up at the red-haired man.

"How dare you! How dare you lay hands on the Princess of Faery?"

He dismounted and stood before her. "Princess is it? You didn't answer; I took your smile for an invitation."

"Next time wait for the invitation to be explicit," she said, maintaining her dignity despite an unusual fluttering in her belly.

He inclined his head in acknowledgement of her words. "Forgive me, lady, but I couldn't mount and ride away leaving such a fair maiden stranded on a rock in a lake. It would have been churlish."

She relaxed, though the fluttering in her belly continued. "There is nothing to forgive. You did me a kindness. It was unnecessary, but you couldn't know that."

One of his eyebrows rose. "Unnecessary? You intended to fly from yon rock, perhaps?" He peered behind her, as though expecting to find wings.

She ignored the comment.

He shrugged, turned to the horse and rummaged in a saddle bag. His hand emerged with a loaf of brown bread. Taking a sgian dubh from a sheath on his calf, he cut a piece and offered it to her.

"Don't touch that, Rhia!"

The mortal whirled to face Roddy. The faery knight had glided to shore on a light coracle and now leapt to face the man.

"Be at ease, Roddy. He has offered me no harm."

"Still, my princess, you must not taste anything he offers or you will owe him a charm."

"I'm aware of the rules, Sir Rhydderich."

The man stepped back so that he no longer stood between Rhiannon and her guard. He studied Roddy, noted the sheathed sword, and glanced at Rhiannon. "So it is true. You are a faery princess."

"I am and in reward for your chivalry, I grant you one wish."

"Rhia!" scolded Roddy, but she quelled him with a glance.

The mortal knelt before her with lowered eyes. "I have only one request, Fair One," he tilted his head and caught her gaze. "that I might once again gaze upon your beauty. Will you meet me here again?"

Rhiannon's belly somersaulted over her heart. Her knees shook and her mind screamed of danger ... but her heart sang.

"What is your name, mortal?"

"I am called Eoin the Strong by my clan."

"Well, Eoin the Strong, I shall honor your request. Meet me here at the next full moon with a selection of the finest bread your realm has to offer. It may be that I will make an exchange."

Roddy sucked in a sharp breath, but her friend held his silence.

Eoin rose, took Rhiannon's hand and kissed it. "I will be here with bread fit for the Ard Ri himself. And should you choose to grant me a boon, I will treasure it, Fair One."

Rhiannon left her hand in his longer than was strictly required, relishing the rough texture of his palm and the restrained strength of his fingers. Her belly continued to shimmy and tumble, but she controlled her features. At last she withdrew her hand and nodded at the handsome mortal. "Until we meet again, Eoin the Strong."

She strolled to Roddy and allowed her friend and guard to hand her into the tiny coracle.

He turned to Eoin and said, "Have a care, mortal. My princess is fair and generous, but that doesn't mean we all are." The faery prince stepped into the boat and waved it into motion.

Eoin bowed low and then straightened and saluted the coracle. "Until we meet again, Fair One."

4

"*A*nd where were you when my headstrong daughter made such a rash promise?" Alberic, King of Faery, skewered me with an angry gaze. "If she accepts food from that creature, she will bind herself to him and to his world."

"He was beside me, as was his duty," said Rhiannon with aplomb. "He held silence because I commanded his obedience. I am aware of the import of my promise. If you are angry, sire, direct your wrath at me, not my faithful friend."

Alberic spun to face his daughter. "I *am* angry and I *will* deal with you. Right now I'm speaking to a knight in my service. Hold your tongue, wench."

Blood drained from Rhiannon's face, but she stood her ground despite her father's insult. "I am not a wench. I am the Princess of Faery."

A sneer twisted her father's face and Rhiannon flinched as though expecting a blow, but he chose to wound her with words instead. "You are not worthy to be a princess. Despite every advantage, you throw yourself at a mortal like a common nymph. You disgust me. And to think your lady mother gave her life for you. I'm glad she didn't live to see you behave so ... so ... immodestly."

"And what about you, Father?" Rhiannon snapped, anger sizzling in her clipped tones. "Would Mother be proud of the bitter, nasty little man you've become?"

Alberic drew back his arm, but I threw myself between father and daughter and caught the king's wrist.

"Forgive me, sire," I said through clenched teeth, "but I cannot allow harm to come to my princess. Not even from you. Not while I have breath in my body."

"Take your hands off me, youngster, or you may find your breaths very limited indeed."

I released the king's wrist, but remained between Alberic and Rhiannon. "Rhiannon, my princess, please leave. Your father and I have much to discuss."

Rhiannon stiffened ... and then turned and strode from the room.

"Sire, you know I love Rhiannon as a sister," I said, lowering my eyes and bowing my head, "and I am your obedient servant, but knowing her as I do, I believe you would do well not to antagonize her about this."

Alberic's face turned crimson and his eyes narrowed. "*I* should not antagonize *her*?" he said, his voice seething with anger. "When she behaves with such wanton disregard for her station? When she plans to leave Faery to consort with a *mortal*?"

"My king," I said, trying to sooth him with my tone, "you know how headstrong she is. If you oppose her, she may do something we will all regret. Leave her to me. Ignore this assignation. Rhiannon knows her own worth. She won't do anything reckless."

As long as you don't goad her into it, I thought, miserably.

The king glared at me, but nodded. "Fine," he said. "I won't oppose her ... for now. But be warned," he said, "prince or no, if you allow harm to come to my daughter, your life will be forfeit."

I bowed before my king. "I understand, sire. I shall see to it that no harm comes to my princess."

5

---

*R*hiannon paced before the shimmering threshold gate, her richly embroidered blue skirt swishing past the close cropped grass. Her pulse raced at the thought of seeing the handsome mortal again and she fought to steady her breathing.

"Remember, my princess, don't eat anything he offers. Don't even touch the bread he brings," chided Roddy. "The enchantment against mortals tasting faery food or faeries partaking of mortal fare is binding, regardless of your station."

"I'm not a child, Roddy. I know the law."

A deeper, more commanding voice answered. "Yes, but will you obey, obstinate child?"

Rhiannon's face settled into a mask as she turned to face her father. "What are you doing here?"

"I've come to protect my interests and the interests of Faery. I will accompany you as you fulfill your oath to this mortal clod."

"I neither require nor desire your presence."

"What you desire is of no consequence."

Rhiannon turned away from her father to face the portal.

"Such has always been the truth. Roddy! Attend me. The moon has risen, my destiny awaits."

Roddy strode forward to take Rhiannon's hand. "Don't let him goad you into foolish action, Rhia," he whispered. "Please, my princess, if you have any love for me, don't throw your life away. I couldn't bear it."

She met his gaze, smiled sadly, and squeezed his hand. "Whatever happens, Roddy, none of it will be your fault," she answered quietly. "You have been a true friend my whole life. I love you like the brother I never had."

Roddy nodded and looked away. Together, they stepped into the whirlwind.

This time, Rhiannon was ready. As the portal winds tore at her skirts and tangled her hair, she bent them to her will. Holding tight to Roddy's hand she stepped from the shimmering vortex onto the lake's sandy shore.

King Alberic landed on the rock.

A golden pavilion glowed in the moonlight a few paces down the beach from Rhiannon and Roddy's landing point. Rhiannon gazed at the inviting structure and released Roddy's hand. She shook out her skirts, smoothed her tangled locks, and took a deep breath to steady her nerves.

"Don't go inside, Rhia," Roddy pleaded in a gruff whisper. "The barbarian means to trap you."

"Nonsense, Roddy. Eoin has prepared this tent in my honor. Of course I will observe his efforts."

At that moment, the tent flap was thrown back and Eoin the Strong emerged. He strode to Rhiannon and made a courtly bow.

"Welcome, Fair One," he said, a smile lighting his handsome features. "I am honored that you came."

"I gave you my word, mortal. I am bound by the promises I speak."

"And glad I am that you are. Please, come inside and be comfortable. I have brought the bread you requested."

"Rhia, don't," warned Roddy.

She hesitated, but Alberic chose that moment to vanish from the rock and reappear at Rhiannon's side.

"Rhiannon! Stop this nonsense and return with me to Faery at once."

She turned away from her father and placed her hand on Eoin's outstretched arm. "I would love to see what you have prepared for me, Eoin the Strong." She awarded him a dazzling smile before throwing a look of contempt over her shoulder at her father.

Eoin glanced from Rhiannon to the two men, and placed his hand over hers where it rested on his arm. He smiled at her. "This way, Fair One," he said leading Rhiannon to the pavilion. As an afterthought, he called over his shoulder, "You gentlemen are welcome to join us, as well."

6

I followed my princess, my closest friend, into the pavilion the mortal had prepared for her, and my heart sank. Rhiannon was clearly enchanted. She clapped her hands together and turned a slow circle in the center of the warmly lit room, her eyes sparkling with delight.

Loathe though I was to admit it even to myself, Eoin the Strong had prepared a shelter worthy of royalty. Canvas walls were hung with richly embroidered tapestries, some depicting woodland scenes of hounds and foxes, horses and deer, while others showed courtly halls peopled with knights and ladies. Beneath our feet lay the pelts of large animals, bears and wild cats as well as sheep and cattle. Flickering lamps hung from support poles, giving the structure a welcoming glow, and folding camp chairs cushioned with colorful pillows were scattered throughout. But the centerpiece was a large wooden table lavishly decorated with boughs of holly and liberally sprinkled with bright red berries and white mistletoe and bearing enough loaves of bread to feed a small village for a month.

There were round loaves, their golden brown crusts scored in cross-hatch patterns, long narrow loaves, oblong loaves so dark their crust seemed almost black, small bread of every shape imaginable — buns and rolls and scones—and in pride of place a large wreath that had been cut and twisted before baking to display the rich filling inside.

My mouth watered just looking at the display, and I could feel Rhiannon's delight washing against the edges of my mind. I glared at Eoin. This mortal was dangerous.

Eoin drew Rhiannon to the table and led her past, pointing out each type of bread in turn, describing its nature and telling of its creator.

"I am not a baker, myself," he said, giving her a shy smile. "Warriors have little time to develop such homey skills, but my mother and sister made the wreath for you, Fair One. They said to tell you each ingredient was added with love and honor, in the hope of meeting you one day."

He fell to one knee, holding her hand in both of his and gazing up into her lovely face. Adoration shone in his eyes. "Will you partake, Fair One?"

"Rhiannon! No!" shouted her father. "Don't even think of disobeying me in this!"

Rhiannon ignored him. She had eyes only for the mortal at her feet. She stretched out her hand and caressed Eoin's hair, his cheek, finally kneeling to face him, one hand in his, the other resting lightly on his shoulder.

"We come from different worlds, Eoin the Strong," she said, her voice soft, but calm and controlled. "Do you understand what you are asking when you offer me your food?"

He gazed into her eyes with clarity and purpose. "I understand, Fair One," he answered. "I am offering you a home. I am offering to protect and provide for you, to share your bed and your love, to father your children, to accept you into my clan and family. Forever."

She nodded, her expression solemn. "And if I accept, I am

vowing to stay by your side, to forsake my title and inheritance in Faery, to live — and die — as a mortal."

King Alberic moaned, but said nothing more. Ancient magic was at play; her father had no authority over her in this matter ... and he knew it.

My own heart was breaking. With each word, I felt her resolve grow stronger. Rhiannon, my princess, my friend, as close as a sister, was about to choose this mortal over me. Over all of us.

"Rhia," I whispered, her name like a prayer on my lips. "Please don't do this, Rhia. Please don't leave us."

She glanced at me and smiled. Not a bright, happy smile, but a wistful one, tinged with sadness. "You have been my friend and brother, Roddy," she said, "but our childhood is at an end. We will be parted no matter which life I choose. If I remain in Faery, I will be sent across the Eastern Sea to the demesne of the wood elves."

She turned again to face the mortal and her expression softened, became more joyous. "I prefer to choose my own fate." Withdrawing her hand from Eoin's, she stood, leaned over the table, and broke off a piece of the filled wreath. Turning to face King Alberic and myself, she held out her free hand to Eoin, who rose and, accepting it, lifted it to his lips.

"I choose to live as a mortal with Eoin the Strong."

She bit into the piece of filled bread, chewed and swallowed.

A breeze wafted through the pavilion, dimming the lanterns and ruffling our hair. When it had passed and the lanterns once again glowed with steady flames, King Alberic strode to his daughter.

"It is done," he said, shaking his head. "Foolish child. I cannot undo what you have done, though I would if I could. The magic is ancient and beyond my skill."

He turned to the man to whom his only daughter had just

pledged her life. "However, I can and will place a binding enchantment upon your union. If you ever raise a hand in anger to my daughter, she will be returned to me at once, whether she wills it or not. Do you understand this condition?"

Eoin straightened his shoulders and met my king's gaze steadily. "I do."

King Alberic nodded. "Furthermore, your line will continue unbroken until my daughter's true heir is born. A princess of your lineage will return to Faery and take Rhiannon's place as heir to the High King's throne."

Eoin and Rhiannon nodded in unison, though Rhiannon's cheeks reddened at the reference to children.

"Finally," the king continued, "as punishment for his failure to protect my daughter from her own idiocy, Prince Rhydderich Drest Guerthenmach, formerly heir to the throne of Winter is cursed to remain in the mortal world to guard my daughter ..."

"Father! No!" cried Rhiannon. "You cannot punish Roddy for my choice!"

Alberic shouted over her, his words drowning out hers. "... and her line until her true heir shall be delivered to me in Faery," he paused, turning his head to glare at me, "at which time he shall be executed for his crimes."

Rhiannon cast one miserable glance at me and burst into tears. Eoin gathered her into his arms and held her while she sobbed. Over her head, his eyes sought mine and I recognized his regret at having been party to my downfall.

"Rhydderich Drest Guerthenmach," King Alberic said, "you are no longer a citizen of Faery. I strip you of all semblance of your former life. Be a dragon until the end of your days."

I stared at him in horror as my body obeyed his command and ceased to be my own. Agony seared through me as my bones melted and reformed, muscles stretched beyond endurance, skin and hair morphed into scales and wings. I prayed to all the elder gods to end my suffering. *Let me die!* I screamed silently since I had no mouth or tongue to utter the words.

At last the excruciating pain receded. I lay panting at the entrance to the pavilion. I pushed myself upright and found I stood on four scaled legs ending in taloned claws. A huff of surprise escaped my lips ... setting the pavilion aflame.

I retreated into the cool darkness and watched as Eoin carried Rhiannon to safety, Alberic striding out behind them. He smirked at me and said, "One final matter, Rhydderich. You are forbidden to show yourself to any being other than the daughter you currently guard, or those who know of your existence. To all others, you will appear as a child's toy, a plaything of no consequence."

He bowed to all of us as we huddled before the burning pavilion. "Enjoy your new life," he sneered, and disappeared.

The moment he was gone, Rhiannon disentangled herself from Eoin and ran to me. She stopped a few paces away, bowing her head and wringing her hands. "Can you ever forgive me, Roddy?" she whispered.

If I'd still had arms I would have wrapped her in a hug. As it was, I lowered my head, resting it on the ground between my front paws. "There is nothing to forgive, my princess," I said, my new voice sounding rough and gravelly to my ears. "Neither of us had any idea your father was capable of such malicious spite."

Eoin strode over to join us. "I am sorry for your banishment and this curse, Sir Rhydderich. I will do all in my power to make sure that your life with us is as pleasant as may be."

I closed my eyes. I really didn't want to look at the mortal who had caused all this mayhem. "I appreciate the thought, Sir Eoin, but the best thing you can do for me is to make my princess happy. Cherish her, and remember your promise to her father." I opened my eyes and glared at him. "Never raise your hand to her in anger or I will slay you before her father has the chance to spirit her home ... and your children will be left parentless."

Eoin nodded and took Rhiannon's hand. "I swear to you, Rhydderich Drest Guerthenmach, I will give Rhiannon no further cause to rue this day."

I nodded and closed my eyes again, opening them immediately when I felt Rhiannon's arms encircle my neck. At least I would never be separated from her. We would be together forever.

EPILOGUE

"Oh, Roddy," I said, tears stinging my eyes. "I'm so sorry. Grandpa was just horrible."

"Yes," he said quietly, "he was."

"Were they happy? Rhiannon and Eoin?"

Roddy smiled. "Very. Considering how little they knew of each other when they made their choice, they built a good, full life together. They loved each other faithfully to the end of their days. Eoin was as good as his word, never giving Rhiannon cause for grief. And if my princess ever regretted her decision, I never knew it."

He closed his eyes, and I knew he was remembering my foremother.

"Watching Rhiannon, my closest friend, wither and die was the hardest thing I'd ever had to do," he whispered. "She was a princess of Faery. She should have lived forever. Instead, she died in a medieval manor attended only by her eldest grand-daughter so that I could be present as a full-size dragon. Eoin had been dead for many years and she said that she was ready to join him, but I ... I was not ready to be left behind. To be cursed to live without her."

I scooted over to sit beside him and pulled him into a tight embrace. "Thank you," I whispered, and felt him start. "Thank you for waiting through all those centuries ... for me."

He turned in my embrace and kissed my cheek. "You were worth the wait."

He pushed me away and stroked my hair. "I loved Rhiannon as a sister and I grieved to watch her die, but if she hadn't made her choice, if Alberic hadn't cursed me to guard her family, we wouldn't be here now." He raised my hand to his lips and kissed it. "And I'd endure it all again to gain your love, Claire."

He stood and pulled me into a full embrace, kissing me gently, but passionately.

"Evidently all of Faery was correct," he whispered. "The heir of Winter was destined to fall in love with the heir to the High King's throne, only her name wasn't Rhiannon ... it's Claire!"

COPYRIGHT

AMELIA FOX: SPY IN TRAINING

1

My name is Amelia Fox, and I'm a spy. Just like my mom.

Okay, I'm a fifteen-year-old girl, and I don't know for a fact that my mom is a spy, but come on! What else could she be? I mean, no one with a lick of intelligence — and my mom is brilliant — could possibly be content as a corporate accountant for a shoe company. I mean, really? She's got to be a spy. Traveling around the world to boring shoe conventions and factory inspections ... that's just her cover. She's actually making the world safe for truth and justice.

Just like superman. Only quieter.

So quiet in fact that she won't even admit to her family what she's up to, and our family is very small and tight. Just Mom and me and Grammie, who watches over me while Mom's off doing her thing. As Grammie always says, "It's just us girls."

Not that our family was always females only. Dad and Grandpa died together in a plane crash in the Wasatch Mountains of Utah when I was just a baby, so while I know Mom and Grammie miss them, I'm okay. I mean, it's hard to miss people you never knew.

But back to Mom being a spy, while she's never admitted anything, I'm pretty smart, so whether she tells me or not. I know the score.

And today, my suspicions were confirmed. During my first day at my new school of all places.

2

*M*ercer Island Academy was designed as a stately English country manor complete with wrought iron fence enclosing the grounds. Mom dropped me off on my first morning, and I sprinted up the stone steps without a backward glance, pausing only after passing through the high front doors into the entry hall.

A pretty blonde girl dressed in the obligatory uniform of a navy, green, and black plaid skirt, white shirt and navy sweater vest, but with her shirttails hanging out, lingered just inside the front door. She clutched her backpack to her chest like a life-preserver and stared wide-eyed around the entry hall. I joined her in silent observation. Polished hardwood floors, high ceilings, and sweeping staircase. The interior walls were wood. Mahogany, just like Mom's desk at home. Several doors stood guard to the right and left of the staircase — mute sentinels guarding the school's secrets. All tightly closed. A crystal chandelier hung suspended over the center of the foyer, blocking the view up the stairs.

"It's so ... grand," whispered the pretty blonde.

"Yeah, but we're here. We belong." I tore my gaze from the

crystals budding from the chandelier and smiled at her. "I'm Amelia Fox. This is my first day. I'm guessing you're new too?"

Blue eyes fastened on me and a shy smile bloomed. "Uh-huh. Paige Andrews. I'm here on a scholarship, and right now I think they made a huge mistake."

I laughed and butted her with my shoulder. "Hey. You're ahead of me. Somebody *chose* you. I'm just here 'cause Mom can afford to pay."

Paige giggled and her face lost the stressed, tight-stretched look. "Glad to meet you, Amelia. Ready to brave the ranks of Mercer Island Academy?"

"Let's do it."

We nodded to each other and marched to the conservatively clad woman who stood to the left of the stairway under a sign that read "New Students: Last Names A - L."

"Good morning, ladies. I'm Miss Wentworth, a guidance counselor here at the academy. What are your names?" She glanced at her clipboard and flipped pages until she found Paige and then me. Pulling sheets from under the clip, she handed one to each of us.

"Here are your schedules. Keep them handy until you've memorized your class assignments and locations," she instructed in clipped tones. "First, though, proceed up the stairs and to the left to the grand ballroom. Headmistress Patrick will address the school in a few minutes."

Paige and I skipped up the stairs and followed a crowd of uniform-clad kids to the ballroom. The large room was set up as an auditorium, complete with temporary stage and rows of folding chairs.

We settled into adjoining chairs and Paige grabbed my schedule to compare classes. I slipped my backpack under my seat, then peered at the pieces of paper in her hand.

"Look! We have English Lit and Algebra together," Paige said.

"Nice. Too bad we have different Social Studies teachers."

"Look at your schedule after lunch!" Paige exclaimed. "Your whole afternoon is dedicated to *Independent Study*." She glanced at me sideways. "Are you some kind of genius, or something? I've got normal classes all day."

I shrugged. "I'm smart, but I bet everyone here is. No idea what that's all about. Guess I'll find out this afternoon."

3

*P*aige and I were just finishing our lunch — Chicken Alfredo with a side of peas and carrots, followed by Peach Melba for dessert — when Miss Wentworth appeared behind Paige.

"Miss Fox," she said, pinning me to my chair with a stern gaze. "Please follow me. We need to arrange your afternoon schedule."

I glanced at Paige, who gave me a wan smile, gathered my dishes onto a tray, and followed the counselor. As we passed a large metal cabinet slotted for trays, I slid the remains of my lunch into an empty slot. Just like we'd been instructed to do when we entered the cafeteria.

Miss Wentworth nodded as I joined her in the hall. "Very good, Miss Fox. You follow directions well." She led me down the main staircase to the entry hall. Pausing before one of the doors I'd noticed earlier, she chose a silver key from a keychain attached to her belt, unlocked it, and gestured me inside.

I hesitated. A locked door. Why would she take me through a locked door? Was I in trouble? I couldn't be in trouble! I hadn't been here long enough to do anything wrong.

Miss Wentworth raised an eyebrow, but remained silent.

I took a deep breath and stepped through into a mahogany paneled hallway that smelled of lemon and beeswax. Miss Wentworth followed me and I heard the lock snick back into place. I suppressed a shudder. Whatever was going on, I was determined to show no fear.

Miss Wentworth's functional low heels clicked on the polished wood floor as we approached the door at the end of the hall. I tried to keep my rubber-soled high-tops from squeaking. My heart was pounding so loudly I was sure the counselor could hear it, and I wanted to keep my noise to a minimum.

As she chose a second key, this one bronze, she said, "If you accept your schedule, you'll be issued the necessary keys."

I frowned. If I accepted my schedule? Like I had a choice?

The door swung open and I peered into a small conference room with white walls and linoleum floors so clean they reflected the furnishings. Plush leather seats were arranged in four rows of five, all facing a glass and steel podium. Four additional leather chairs sat behind the podium, facing the other twenty. Nineteen heads turned to look at me as Miss Wentworth gestured for me to take the final seat in the audience.

I slipped into the soft leather chair and nodded to the girl next to me. She turned back to the podium without acknowledging my presence.

Miss Wentworth stepped to the podium as a door opened near the front and four additional adults entered, filing up to sit behind her. Each adult wore a dark blue Mercer Island Academy blazer. One man — horn-rimmed glasses, a white button-down shirt and a fussy little bow tie — wiped the leather chair with a white handkerchief before sitting down.

The other man — blond hair, blue eyes, white polo shirt, no facial hair — plopped down and studied the ceiling. Which seemed odd, since it was featureless, white acoustic tiles.

The other two female teachers were dressed identically to Miss Wentworth. Dark blue blazers, white blouses, and pleated skirts that fell just below the knee in the same navy, green, and black plaid that the female students wore. Fortunately, our skirts were cut to a more fashionable length.

"Welcome, students," Miss Wentworth said, causing every eye to focus on her. "I'm sure you're all wondering about your afternoon schedules. First, let me say that while Mercer Island Academy is a fine institution of learning, specializing in preparing young people for academic success at the university level, it is also houses a rather specialized program of study accessible only to students who have been recommended by, shall we say, experts in the field."

I glanced around at the other boys and girls in the audience, wondering who they were and what we'd been recommended for.

"Mr. Smith, if you will hand out the schedules, please. Students, refrain from opening your envelopes until I give you permission."

The blond man stepped forward, accepted a stack of manila envelopes from Miss Wentworth and, checking the name on each, handed them to individual students. Most of us frowned and looked puzzled on inspecting the envelope, and when I finally received mine, I understood why.

The name on the outside was *C. Bedelia.*

My mouth fell open, but I stifled a protest. No way would I open the envelope since it clearly wasn't mine.

Miss Wentworth cleared her throat, drawing our attention back to the front of the room.

"I assure you, Mr. Smith has not made a mistake in handing you that particular envelope. You have each been recommended by someone the Mercer Island Academy trusts to be enrolled in our, uh, *unique* program of study. You have been chosen to be trained for covert operations, as spies, and as such each of you will be known by your cover, your *legend*, rather than by your true identity."

My heart went into overdrive. I *knew* it! I knew Mom was a spy, and here was the proof. She'd enrolled me in a private school and recommended me for spy training! I grinned down at the envelope and wondered who *C. Bedelia* was supposed to be and what she was going to learn this year?

"If any of you would prefer not to be involved in this program, you are free to leave the room now," Miss Wentworth continued. "Do not open your envelope. Simply leave it on your chair and exit by the door you came in through. Someone will escort your back to the office and your schedule will be updated there. You will, of course, be required to sign a non-disclosure agreement."

She paused, but no one moved.

Leave? Now? As if!

"Excellent," said Miss Wentworth. "Your training begins now. You will be given half an hour to study your schedule and memorize your legend. Do you understand, Miss Bedelia?"

A heartbeat of silence followed, then my brain caught up and I realized Miss Wentworth had asked me a question. *I was Miss Bedelia.*

"Yes, Miss Wentworth," I said in a clear voice. "I understand."

"Very good." She nodded to Mr. Horn-rimmed Glasses, who pulled a stop watch from his pocket. "Begin timing ... now!"

I ripped open my envelope with shaking fingers, more excited to be *C. Bedelia* than I'd ever been to be Amelia Fox. I yanked a sheaf of papers out and absorbed their contents.

I was Claire Bedelia, a fifteen-year-old girl from Montpelier, Vermont.

Seriously? Vermont? I was Seattle born and bred. I had no

idea what a Vermonter sounded like. Would I lose credit for having the wrong accent?

No time to worry now. I only had half an hour to memorize this stuff.

My father, Gerald, was an attorney specializing in family law, my mom, Stacy, a stay-at-home mom. I smiled. Stacy. Stay-at-home. I could remember that. My ten-year-old brother, Charlie, was nuts about dinosaurs. *You have a brother. Remember that.* I was an only child in real life, so I had no experience with siblings, younger or older.

Claire was an avid soccer fan, loved horses, and dreamed of becoming a veterinarian. Gag!

I memorized details of Claire's (my) life and, with five minutes left, turned to my schedule. Mornings would remain in the larger school, picking up subjects required by the state, but my afternoons would be spent in training for covert operations.

Monday, Wednesday, and Friday afternoons would focus on Beginning Chinese, Code Breaking 101, and Self-Defense for Novices. Tuesdays and Thursdays I'd attend World Geography for Covert Forces, Introduction to Urdu, and Basic Weapons Training.

A huge grin spread across my face. This was real. I was going to learn about weapons and code breaking. I could hardly wait to get home, hug Mom, and promise never to give her attitude again for the rest of my life! This was a dream-come-true.

"Time!" called Miss Wentworth. "Mr. Jones, please collect the data and destroy it."

Horn-rimmed Glasses guy came around and we handed him our papers. I gave mine up willingly, but I noticed a couple of people still reading as the information was pulled from their grasping fingers.

"Attention please," Miss Wentworth said. The room quieted and we all stared avidly forward. "Let me explain the rules of our program. As soon as you walk through that door, you will leave your normal self behind. You will become your legend. No other student in this program will know your real name. Your schedules have been arranged so that you will not be in any non-covert classes together. However, if you should bump into one another in the hallway or encounter each other in the cafeteria, you will walk away with as few words as possible. You will not act in such a way as to raise suspicion in your civilian classmates, but you will avoid each other as completely as possible."

She waited for that command to sink in before continuing. "Also, some of you may believe that you know who recommended you for this program. Trust me; you do not. Under no circumstances will you say or do anything to cause anyone, sponsor or not, to suspect that your school day is anything other than what the civilian population of Mercer Island Academy experiences."

I shifted in my seat, suddenly uncomfortable. I really wanted to talk to Mom about all this. Evidently I wasn't the only one with issues. The room was suddenly alive with the rustle of clothes and the squeaks of distressed leather.

"This is not open to negotiation," said Miss Wentworth. "Failure to obey this rule will result in your expulsion from Mercer Island Academy. Not just the covert program, the academy in general. Do I make myself clear?"

We murmured our assent, and the room fell silent.

"At the end of this school year, if your sponsor is in a position to do so, he or she may choose to reveal himself or herself to you. However, please understand, that the decision is your sponsor's ... and his or hers alone. You may never be told who recommended you. Learn to live with not knowing."

For the rest of the afternoon we solidified our legends by introducing ourselves to each other and reciting our new identities. Finally, in the last half-hour of the school day, we were assigned to pods. Each of the five adults would be mentoring four students. My pod, code name: sea lions, would be under Miss Wentworth's watchful eye.

Before we were dismissed for the day, Miss Wentworth issued our keys. "Silver for the entry hall door," she said, "bronze for the door to this room. Tomorrow you'll be escorted into the classroom and laboratory section. Plan to arrive early. You'll need time for orientation. Any questions?"

I raised my hand. "Just one. Why keys? Wouldn't cards and card readers be simpler?"

She nodded. "They would. They would also be less secure. You see, while you might think that these locks could be picked easily, you'd be mistaken. The keys are of different metals for a reason. The lock mechanism reads the chemical composition of the key as well as whether or not the teeth fit the tumblers. Anyone attempting to use a copy would find themselves in trouble in very short order."

"Wow," said the other girl in our pod, code name: Nancy.

"Wow, indeed," agreed Miss Wentworth. "Now, guard your keys. They're coded to you, so if a set shows up in someone else's possession, we'll know who the careless party was."

Four heads nodded solemnly.

"Very good. You've had a long first day. Mark, Nancy, Sheldon, and Claire, I'm looking forward to training you. Go home. Sleep well. Commit nothing to paper or pixels, and remember who you are at all times during the day tomorrow."

"Thank you, Miss Wentworth," I said, and using my bronze key for the first time, slipped into the mahogany paneled hall.

4

That was the beginning of the hardest and best school year of my life.

Every morning I arrived at school as Amelia Fox, best friend of Paige Andrews. After lunch, Paige ran down a hall to chemistry while her best friend Amelia disappeared to a carrel in a special section of the research library to study the mathematical theorems involved in population health. A topic no sane teenager would want quiz me on.

In reality, I used my silver key to step through a door in the entry hall, morphing from Seattleite Amelia into Claire Bedelia, a Vermont girl who adored her little brother and carried his picture with her everywhere.

As the year progressed, our pod began to speak Chinese during our weekly sessions with Miss Wentworth. On rare occasions she would switch to Urdu and anyone who didn't follow the transition was sentenced to remedial classes after school.

Weapons training was a mixed bag. I'd never be a whiz with bow and arrow, but give me a Sig Sauer pistol and I could break it down, clean it, and put it back together fully loaded with the safety on faster than anyone else in my class. I was even a decent shot.

But code breaking was my favorite class. My brain understood codes. I could look at a coded transcript and literally see the letters and numbers rearrange themselves before my eyes.

Evidently, this was expected.

"Your sponsor told us to expect you to be a natural at code breaking," Mr. Jones said after I'd aced a particularly difficult exam. "And I must say, you haven't disappointed. I'm very pleased with your work, Miss Bedelia."

"Thank you, sir."

While not a class, as such, we also learned highly effective methods of memorization, because nothing we were working on was allowed to leave our section. No papers. No computers, laptops, tablets, or cell phones. Claire Bedelia did not exist beyond the door with the silver key and neither did her studies.

One interesting sidelight of this restriction was that as I became an ace at recollection, I worked on expanding my retentive capacity by gathering intelligence on my fellow students. First I found the members of my pod and surreptitiously learned their real names and personal data. Nothing written, of course, and nothing obvious. Even Paige, who spent nearly every minute of my non-covert day by my side, never noticed me observing classmates.

Like code breaking, intelligence gathering came as naturally as breathing.

By the end of the school year, I could have told Miss Wentworth anything she wanted to know about any member of my covert pod. Of course, I didn't. If she wanted the information, she'd have to ask. I'd already decided that next year, I'd set my sights on learning about the upperclassmen. So far, I'd only caught the occasional glimpse of an older covert ops student, but next year, they'd be on my radar.

And so, as my first successful year of spy training ended, I looked forward to finally having a long talk with Mom. I could hardly wait to tell her everything I'd learned and to hear a little bit about what she actually did. Not the boring balance sheets and stock reports that were her legend, but the exotic places she'd been, the important intelligence she'd gathered.

Because I knew my mom was a spy, just like I was becoming, and I knew without a doubt that once the first year restriction was lifted, she'd want to talk to me just as badly as I wanted to talk to her.

5

*W*hen the last bell rang on the final day of school I bounded out to the car, too excited for words. Mom and I could finally talk!

Only Mom wasn't behind the wheel of our midnight blue Mercedes coupe. Grammie was driving. I shelved my disappointment, climbed into the front passenger seat, and asked, "Where's Mom?"

Grammie watched me buckle up before answering. "She had that convention in Geneva, remember? Her flight left at noon." She flipped on her turn signal and moved slowly, carefully into traffic.

"I remember," I said with a sigh, "but I thought she was leaving tomorrow."

"That was the plan until her administrative assistant called with an updated schedule."

"Oh. Okay."

"So, how was your last day?" Grammie asked. "In fact, I haven't heard enough about your whole year. Now that it's over, I want to hear everything." The car slid to a stop at a traffic light and Grammie and I looked at each other.

No, I thought. *It couldn't be!*

Grammie chuckled. "Had you fooled, didn't I? You thought your mother sponsored you."

"Seriously?" I asked. "It was you?" My heart plummeted, taking my mood with it. "Mom didn't think I was good enough?"

The light changed, but Grammie didn't move the car forward. "Oh, sweetie!" she said, as a horn blared from the car behind us. "Just a sec."

Grammie pulled across the intersection and into a convenience store parking lot. She killed the motor, then turned to face me.

"Amelia Fox, your mother loves you with all her heart. If she'd been able or had known anything about this program, she would've recommended you in a heartbeat."

I blinked back the tears that had been threatening to fall and stared at Grammie. "What do you mean, 'if she'd known'?"

Grammie beamed. "Sweetheart, your mom isn't a spy, has never been a spy. She didn't have what it took and your grandfather and I knew that. We never recommended her for training."

"You and Grandpa?" I asked. This couldn't be true. But how else would she know about the training program, about my needing a recommendation? "Y...you were spies?"

"Indeed we were," she said, nodding exuberantly. "Two of the best. And you father was a CIA analyst. He wasn't a field operative, was never interested in that aspect, but he finished the training and could break code faster than anyone else in the service." She smiled at me. "Pretty sure you take after him in that department."

My mind whirled. Mom was a civilian, but Grammie and Grandpa and my dad had all been spies. Code breaking was in my blood ... just not from whom I expected.

"So, Mom doesn't know anything about the covert operations department at Mercer Island Academy?"

Grammie shook her head. "Not a blessed thing, and we're going to keep it that way, aren't we?"

I thought about my plans for the upperclassmen next year, and how I'd be expelled if I told a civilian about my studies. I loved my mom, but I loved my training too.

"She won't hear it from me," I promised.

"Good girl," said Grammie, "but now that you know I sponsored you, you can tell me all about your adventures. I'd love to hear who's teaching you and what kind of assignments you're being given."

I breathed out a happy sigh and nodded. I could hardly wait to tell her!

EPILOGUE

Okay, so I was wrong. My mom's not a spy.

But my grandmother is, and I'm a spy-in-training.

Now that I have a confidant to share my successes and failures with, I really excited for my next year of training to begin. But for right now, Grammie and I have a lot of catching up to do before Mom gets home from Geneva!

Can life get any better?

I can hardly wait to find out!

COPYRIGHT

THE CASE OF THE MISSING INARIAN

SPACE STATION DETECTIVE

*M*y name is Cinnamon Chou, and I'm a detective.

Okay, I'm a kid, but I'm going to be a detective when I grow up. Just like my dad. For now, I'm practicing on the easy stuff. You know, like lost full-spectrum goggles ("They're perched on top of your head, Master Engineer Wyandotte"), missing red silk slippers ("Got 'em, Mrs. Abrega! When was the last time you cleaned under your bed?"), or my favorite, *The Case of the Missing Inarian*.

What's an Inarian? I'm glad you asked.

An Inarian is a warm-blooded denizen of the planet Inaria. They're cute and cuddly and definitely don't meet the standard of intelligence necessary to classify them as Class I Sapient Beings. Reading through my data links on old Earth biology, I've decided they're pretty similar to hamsters. They make great pets, but they're about as bright as deep space with no stars in sight.

My best friend, Lando Maxon, has an Inarian named Dumpling. When Lando woke up that morning, he discovered that Dumpling had managed to escape from his habitat. Inarians may not be smart, but they can wriggle out of places you'd swear were tightly sealed.

Normally, a Dumpling escape wouldn't merit my intervention as a detective. Lando would just set out a bowl of Dumpling's favorite treats and wait for his pet to get hungry. But today was not a normal day. Today Lando and his family were leaving the space station and returning to Centauri Three, their home planet.

That's one of the real bummers about living on a space station. Sooner or later all of your friends move away.

Of course, the up side is that new friends cycle in constantly.

At least, that's what my mom tells me every time a close friend leaves for a distant star system. Dad says Mom is an optimist. He's right, but so is she. By the time I grow up and take my place in the Universal Star League, I'll have friends in so many star systems I'll need my own database just to keep track of them all.

Back to Dumpling. I was eating breakfast with Mom and Dad when Lando pinged my link. "Lando Maxon," my link announced.

Mom frowned at the link on my wrist. "Not at the table, Cinnamon," she said, using her duty officer voice. "You know the rules."

I swallowed a mouthful of protein-rich, calcium-enhanced syntho-juice, wiped my mouth on a recycled napkin and said, "But Mom, Lando is leaving the station in less than six hours. If I don't answer him, I may not have another chance."

Mom glanced at Dad, who nodded.

"Very well, Cinnamon," she said, "Your father and I will make an exception this time. You are dismissed."

I grabbed a slice of replicated toast, jumped out of my chair, and dashed for the door. I didn't want to give Mom time to reconsider.

Not that she would. Decisions were Mom's life. As a senior officer assigned to the bridge of Space Station Zeta, Mom made hundreds of decisions. She was awesome. Cool and professional, with nerves of steel. Nobody messed with Mom.

She was also beautiful, in a cool and commanding kind of way. Sleek black hair, dark chocolate skin, and eyes as green as all-clear lights. She had a spacer's body, tall and willowy, but tough as nano-enhanced titanium.

Dad, a detective assigned to station security, was a genetic throw-back. Despite being born on Cygnus 12, his DNA identified him as ethnic Chinese. He wasn't exactly short, but he wasn't tall and willowy like Mom. Dad had a compact strength, like a compressed spring. And smart. Oh yeah. Dad's brain held onto facts like a super-computer, but with the ability to make intuitive leaps that computers still hadn't mastered.

Me? Dad says I'm the best of both of them. I've got Dad's thought-processing brilliance combined with Mom's decision-making skills. I just need time to develop my intuition and experience to feed my knowledge base.

I'm also a genetic combination. Where Mom is dark-skinned and Dad is gold-hued, I'm ... well, cinnamon skin-toned. That's where I got my name. Dad took one look at me and said, "She's perfect, Maria. Our own little cinnamon sugar cookie."

Fortunately for me, they dropped the cookie reference and left it at Cinnamon. I'm cool with that. Nothing wrong with being named after an old world spice. Cinnamon might have been common back on old Earth, but out here in space, it's exotic. I like being exotic.

Once I escaped our quarters and made it into the corridor, I answered Lando's ping.

"What's up, Lando? Need help packing?"

A tiny 3-D model of my friend hovered above my wrist link. It was hard to tell on such a miniscule face, but I thought he looked worried.

"Kinda ... maybe. Look, it's Dumpling. He escaped again.

Only this time I don't have time to wait for him to come out of hiding."

I nodded, thoughts racing. "Plus, I'll bet your quarters haven't been sealed. Not with everyone packing and moving boxes to the landing bay."

"He could be anywhere," Lando agreed.

"I'm on my way." I paused, thinking about my approach to the case. "Does your family have a DNA detector?"

The tiny Lando shrugged. "Maybe, but if we do, it would've been packed long ago. Not exactly a necessity."

"Gotcha," I replied. "I'll ask Dad to borrow his. See you in a few. Cinnamon Chou, over and out."

I ended the link, but before I could return to our quarters, Dad stepped into the corridor.

"Just the person I needed to see," I said, giving him my brightest smile.

Dad cocked an eyebrow, glanced from my dazzling smile to the finger hovering above my link and said, "What do you need, sugar cookie? Or rather, what does Lando need?"

I grimaced. Only Dad could get away with comparing me to an overly sweet pastry. "Lando's Inarian has escaped and he doesn't have time to wait for it to reappear on its own."

Dad nodded. "You're hoping for a DNA detector?"

I upped the wattage on my smile and nodded.

"I don't know, Cinnamon. Those are delicate instruments, easily misread."

My smile morphed into a scowl in a nanosecond. "Really, Dad? You think I'd mistake Inarian DNA for, oh, I don't know, a Tenarian tunnel rat?"

Dad had the grace to drop his gaze. "No. I know you'd use it properly." He sighed, stared at the ceiling for a moment, then nodded. "Follow me, Detective Chou."

My grin returned, and I skipped down the corridor at Dad's heels.

Space station corridors can be very confusing. A person new to the station often thinks they all look alike, but they're wrong. You just have to get used to the subtle clues. Since I've grown up on Space Station Zeta, I'm never lost. I can tell purple sector from blue without even having to resort to the colored chips embedded in the corridor walls and floors. I can tell the sectors by their odors.

Green sector houses hydroponics and smells of nutrients, water and growing plants. Purple sector houses the market district. Purple always smells of hot oil, spices, and too many humans and aliens packed into too little space. Red sector is mechanical engineering. If you think nanobots and computer circuitry don't have distinct odors, then you've never lived on a space station.

And then there's white sector. Medics and remedies; antiseptics and bile; with a stiff overlay of fear. I shivered. I hated even walking past white sector.

But now I followed Dad to my favorite sector: blue. Blue sector is administration, which translates to military since Space Station Zeta is a Universal Star League station. As such the station is under the command and protection of the USL Fleet. Both of my parents are USL officers, so blue sector smells of peace, security, and home.

Not that we lived in blue sector. All living quarters were in the central core — yellow sector. Yellow was further divided into crew and civilian quarters, and then by individual or family, but beyond that our station had no class boundaries. At least not where living quarters were concerned.

Dad paused before the entrance to security, waited for the station to acknowledge his voice and retinal prints, and then strode inside when the entry irised open. I followed quickly. The door would've irised open for me as well, but why wait to be scanned when I could just stick close to Dad?

Everyone but me wore blue and silver USL uniforms. The officers, like Dad, with insignia of rank emblazoned on chest and shoulder, the crew with the simple, stylized USL logo. Everyone saluted when Dad entered, since he was the ranking officer. When he returned their salute, they relaxed and called greetings to me as well.

"Aikens," Dad called, and a young man snapped to attention. "Please find an old DNA detector for Cinnamon. It doesn't need to be state-of-the-art," he continued, "just functional."

"Sir. Yes, sir."

Dad cocked a brow at me. "What are you waiting for, Detective Chou? Follow Aikens, collect your gear, and get out of my office."

I grinned, saluted, and ran to follow Aikens. I found him in the supply closet, rummaging through a box of outdated gear.

"What are you up to today, Cinnamon?" he asked as he rooted through the box. "Why a DNA detector?"

"My friend is cycling off-station today, and his Inarian escaped. I'm hoping to help him track it down before he ships out."

Aikens paused, dislodged a small electronic device, and pulled it free of the box. Thumbing it on, he checked the read-out, then nodded.

"This should do the trick," he said, handing the detector to me. "It's got plenty of juice and is reading properly. Good luck with your search."

"Thanks! This should make it easy." I saluted Aikens, ran back past Dad's office and out into the station corridor. Now to get to Lando's quarters on the double.

I arrived at the Maxon family quarters in yellow sector sweaty and out of breath.

"Hi ... Mrs. Maxon ..." I wheezed. "Is ... Lando ... home?"

Lando's mother gave me a distracted look and waved toward Lando's room. "He's in his room. Searching for Dumpling."

I nodded. "I heard," I said, my breathing settling into a more normal pattern. "I'm here to help."

She turned back to the wardrobe she was inventorying. "I hope you can. We won't be able to delay our departure for an Inarian."

"Understood," I said, already on my way to join my friend. As the door whooshed open and I stepped into Lando's room, he raced forward, grabbed my hand and pulled me to the habitat.

"I think I've found where he got out," he said, pointing to a junction between the main habitat and one of the tubular trails that allowed Dumpling to roam the edges of Lando's room. "That connection is slightly loose. It doesn't look wide enough for escape, but it's the only possibility I've found."

I got down on my hands and knees to examine the evidence. Sure enough, Lando had discovered a half-inch gap between the main habitat and the tube.

Now Inarians are small, but they're not *that* small. Dumpling was at least six inches long, but while he looked like he was as round as he was long, he was actually little more than a walking ball of fluff. I'd seen him squeeze himself flat under his exercise wheel. No idea why he'd done that, but I'd witnessed it with my own two eyes. If he could get into that tiny space, he could ooze out through the loose connection Lando had discovered.

I pulled the DNA detector out of my pocket and turned it on.

"Okay," I said, "this device is our best hope. Look around and find me a bit of his fur or blood, or, well, whatever might have his DNA."

I examined the escape point to see if he might have scraped himself and left a sample behind, but the smooth edges were clear. A whoop of victory told me that Lando had fared better.

"Here, Cinnamon. I found a clump of fur."

I held my breath as we touched the DNA detector's probe to the fur. "Let there be DNA," I whispered. "Let there be DNA." I knew enough about genetics to know that unless a hair has the follicle or root attached, you can't get a DNA reading. I watched the meter's read-out. Nothing.

Carefully, I touched a different bit of the fur with the probe ... and the screen lit. We had a reading!

Lando said, "Yes!" and I exhaled in relief.

"Now what?" he asked.

"Now we follow Dumpling's DNA trail." I worked the dials on the device and locked in the sample reading. Now the screen would only light when matching DNA was detected.

Crawling along Lando's bedroom floor, we followed the trace evidence Dumpling had left behind. The trail led to a very small hole in the wall between Lando's bedroom and the main room of the family's quarters.

I glanced at Lando and saw his shoulders sag. He was thinking the same thing I was ... what if Dumpling found a way to scurry along inside the walls? We'd never be able to track him through the permaplastic.

After a quick discussion of our options, we agreed that Lando would stay in his room beside the hole, while I ran into the main room to see if there was an exit anywhere nearby.

I laid the DNA detector on the floor and tapped the wall, hoping to hear Lando tapping back. There! I was about six feet too far into the room. I moved toward his rappings, pleased to hear the noise getting louder. When I found the right place, I lay down on my stomach and searched the junction of floor and wall.

"Lando!" I shouted into the little hole. "I found it. There's a matching hole on this side."

"Did he come through?" Lando yelled back. "Does the DNA

trail continue?"

Rats! Or maybe I should say, Inarians! The detector was several feet away on the floor where I'd left it. I jumped up to retrieve it, just in time to see a loading dock worker push a floating cargo cart into the room. He'd come to collect some of the Maxons' belongings, and he stopped the cart right over the DNA detector.

If he allowed the cart to settle, he'd crush the instrument that was our only hope of finding Dumpling in time!

"No!" I yelled. "Don't settle the cart there. You'll crush my gadget."

The dock worker stared at me, then checked around his feet, clearly confused. He was just about to lower the cart when I pulled a Dumpling and threw myself into the space under the cart. The way too small space to accommodate my bulk.

"What the..." the worker said, and steered the cart into the center of the room, away from my flying feet and fingers. "Are you nuts, kid? This thing could break you in half."

I grabbed the detector and hugged it close to my hammering heart. "I know," I answered, "but it would've pulverized my DNA detector."

Shaking his head at the lunacy of kids, the dock worker settled the cargo cart and began loading it with boxes.

Moving back to the hole in the wall, I sank to the floor, closed my eyes, and allowed myself to simply breathe until Lando joined me.

"Well?" he asked. "Do we have a trail, or don't we?"

I held the detector out to him. "You check," I said. "I'm still recovering from a close encounter."

He cocked his head and gave me a quizzical expression, silently asking for an explanation, but I waved him toward the hole. I'd tell him all about it later, in a cyber-sending if not in person.

Lando bent to the floor and a moment later gave a fist pump. "We have a trail," he cried and crawled off toward the family kitchen.

Thanks to Dad's old DNA detector, we found Dumpling fifteen minutes later curled up in an empty kitchen cabinet, surrounded by bits of breakfast cereal. The cabinet door was firmly latched, with no cracks big enough for even the flattest Inarian to wriggle through.

Lando and I decided that Dumpling must have already been in the cabinet when Mrs. Maxon gave the kitchen a final once-over and closed the door.

With the over-full Inarian still sleeping off his cereal high, Lando and I set about disassembling his habitat and packing it for the journey. Dumpling would be confined to a small carry-case for the duration, but he seemed blissfully unconcerned.

I walked my best friend and his family to the loading dock. Not the cargo loading dock. The people loading dock. There wasn't much to see, just a little waiting room with a door that led into a tube. It reminded me of Dumpling's tubular trail system, only this tube would carry my best friend in the whole universe to the space ship that would take him from our home on Space Station Zeta to his new home on Centauri Three.

I wasn't sure how many light years would separate us, but it really didn't matter. Too many to bridge with a tubular trail.

The light over the exit turned green, and passengers began to move slowly to the tube.

Mr. and Mrs. Maxon each hugged me and thanked me again for rescuing Dumpling ... and thereby their son. Then they stepped aside so Lando could approach.

"Well," he said, staring at his shoes, "I guess this is it, Cinnamon."

"Yeah," I sighed. "I guess so." I looked at the floor, too, willing the tears not to flow.

"Thanks for being my friend." He touched my hand, and suddenly my arms were around him, hugging him tight.

"You'll always be my friend," I whispered, my throat tight with tears I didn't want to shed. "Light years can't change that."

He nodded and we stepped apart.

"Take care of Dumpling for me," I said. Then a thought struck. "Here. Take this." I thrust the DNA detector into his hands. "It's old and Dad doesn't need it ... and you never know when you might need to track an Inarian."

Lando smiled, brushed the back of his hand across his eyes, and said, "Thanks, Cinnamon. You're the best."

A moment later Lando and his parents disappeared into the tube. I stood there staring at the empty passageway until a blue and silver clad security crewmember closed and locked the door.

I walked away from the dock, heading back to tell Dad what had happened to his DNA detector, when I heard a woman speaking. A woman who sounded like she was trying to be excited but was failing rather spectacularly.

Turning, I saw a tall, willowy blonde woman in the blue and silver of the USL leading a blue-eyed girl with light brown hair pulled into braids. "Don't worry, Sammy. I'm sure we'll be happy here. You'll make friends in no time, and I ... I'll learn my new post quickly. Everything is going to be A-Okay."

She raised her eyes, saw me watching, and gave a little wave. "See, honey? There's a little girl about your age. Maybe she can help us find our quarters."

I straightened my shoulders, pasted on a smile, and walked over to the newcomers. This Sammy person might not be able to replace Lando, but I could definitely help them find their quarters.

After all, Space Station Zeta was my home, and I was a detective. I could find *anything*!

COPYRIGHT

THE WARBIRDS OF
ABSAROKA

PROLOGUE

*J*ohn Standing Bear lay upon his deathbed. Though his eyes were closed, he was aware of the fading sunlight streaming through his bedroom window, felt the cool breeze freshen the stale air in a room kept overly warm to comfort a dying man. His lips twitched in a half smile. He had sat death-watch for many a brave warrior. Now his turn had come to be watched.

His body felt oddly light. Perhaps he no longer perceived it properly, perhaps his spirit had already begun to detach itself from his flesh. And yet, an anchor remained. His granddaughter sat beside him, a quiet presence. She remained silent, but gently stroked his right hand, letting him know she was there.

"Granddaughter," he whispered. The word held little substance, like a breath of wind barely stirring the aspen leaves in the high mountain valley of his birth, so long ago on Earth. He had grown to manhood in that valley, had loved it fiercely. But he had chosen to leave Earth behind, had been instrumental in founding the colony on this planet, on his beloved Absaroka.

Brenna squeezed his fingers, bringing him back to the task at hand: dying.

"I am here, Grandfather."

He marshaled his strength for a final act of will. He must pass on his warning, must know that Brenna understood. His people had forgotten the horrors of war with an alien species. He had not. To them, the bug-eyed monsters were merely a cautionary tale written of in history books, but to John, the memories were real. He had served on the *USL Ascension*, had experienced the heart-stopping fear as the ship battled for its life and the lives of humanity. The Bug-Eyes had withdrawn all those years ago, but he knew with a certainty he could never explain that they would return. And when they did, Absaroka must be prepared to defend herself. Brenna must understand.

"Do not," he wheezed, each word an effort, "allow them ... to remain ... complacent." It was difficult to control his breathing, hard to draw enough breath to push out a word. Light sparkled beyond his closed eyes. So beautiful. So free. All he needed was to let go.

Not yet. Not until she acknowledged his words. He must pass the baton to his grandchild. She must keep knowledge of the enemy alive.

"The Bug-Eyes..." More words refused to come. His breath failed; his strength had ebbed.

Brenna stroked his hand again. He focused his remaining attention on her words. "Be at ease, Grandfather," she said, her voice calm and reassuring. "I am on guard, and you have taught me well. I will build a fleet to defend Absaroka."

John tried to nod, but the effort was too much. His work was done. The fate of Absaroka rested in Brenna's hands now. A dry exhalation escaped his lips and he released his spirit to join his ancestors..

1

---

*B*renna Standing Bear waited for her turn to address the Planetary Council. Though her face wore a mask of calm, her stomach roiled, making her wish she had not eaten even her usual light breakfast of tea and buttered toast with honey. Her palms were moist and she longed to rub them dry on her slim black skirt, but she refused to betray her emotions with such a noticeable act. She closed her eyes, exhaled slowly and willed herself to be calm. Feeling more in control, she opened her eyes and surveyed the chamber.

The Longhouse was crowded, the Confederated Nations of Absaroka were well represented. Brenna nodded, pleased. She wanted as many of her people as possible to hear her words, to understand her grandfather's warning.

Unlike the traditional Earth buildings for which it had been named, Absaroka's Longhouse was a gleaming multistory building of glass and plasteel. The seat of government for the Confederated Nations, the edifice held offices for the leaders of each of the one hundred and forty-seven tribes that had chosen to band together to establish this new world more than eighty years before. The central chamber where the Planetary Council now met was designed to hold several thousand onlookers. Rows of tiered seats rose in semi-circular waves around a large central platform where the representatives of each founding nation sat to discuss matters of global significance. The Long-house also housed several smaller council chambers, miniature versions of the central chamber, for use by smaller groups to consider tribal or regional concerns.

Though Brenna sat on the central platform, she had no official place on the Planetary Council. She was a guest, tolerated because of her grandfather's reputation and influence. She had petitioned to speak before the council, and because John Standing Bear's memory was to be honored at today's meeting, his granddaughter would be indulged.

Councilman Jason Wolfclaw opened the meeting. "The Confederated Nations of Absaroka meet today to honor a great man. John Standing Bear was instrumental in choosing this planet, founding the original colony, and helping Absaroka gain admittance to the Universal Star League. Because of his service, Absaroka is defended by USL ships. Because of his sacrifice, Universal Star League acknowledges the courage and fortitude of Absaroka's warriors and welcomes them into the USL Academy. John Standing Bear's wise counsel will be sorely missed."

Councilwoman Amanda Silverfox rose as Councilman Wolf-claw resumed his seat.

Brenna's stomach jumped and flipped like a fish pulled from clear water. The councilwoman would introduce her. She prayed that the Great Spirit would direct her words, that He would open the ears of the council to heed her grandfather's warning. She sought strength and calm as the councilwoman's words washed over her.

"...John Standing Bear's only surviving descendent. Please give your attention to Sister Brenna Standing Bear."

Her moment had come. Brenna rose to face the council,

smoothing her skirt and discreetly tugging her black, military-style jacket into place.

"Thank you, Elder Silverfox." She inclined her head in acknowledgement of the councilwoman. Her eyes swept over the members of the Planetary Council, then she turned to the audience, her people, the ones her grandfather had always sought to protect.

"My grandfather was a great man." Murmurs of assent whispered through the chamber. "He worked tirelessly to protect Absaroka. To protect you." Heads nodded all around her. "Even as he lay dying, his thoughts were of his people. Though he was one hundred and fifteen years old, an age at which most men would have laid down their burdens, Grandfather was still concerned with the safety and viability of this planet. With *your* continued safety."

A quiet mutter of discontent reached her from the council members behind her. She turned to face them, the decision makers. The men and women who held the fate of Absaroka in their hands.

"Grandfather believed passionately in the need to establish a fleet of ships to defend Absaroka, and I agree. We cannot rely utterly on the USL for our defense. We must establish a planetary militia and arm it with a fleet of space worthy vessels. We must be prepared to defend Absaroka."

Quiet murmuring grew to a din a raised voices. Her people voiced their opinions, both for and against her assertions. Brenna stood quietly, aware that her voice would not carry above the swelling roar. She assessed the mood. Many supported her, but as she had expected, just as many disagreed.

When the crescendo of voices reached its peak, Brenna became aware of a gavel pounding on plasteel. She turned again to the council and saw Principal Chief Winona Old Coyote standing and applying the gavel vigorously. Gradually, the chamber quieted.

Principal Chief Old Coyote eyed Brenna thoughtfully. A diminutive, silver-haired woman, Winona Old Coyote exuded authority. She listened attentively and spoke infrequently, but when she did, her words carried weight. The Principal Chief had been a good friend to John Standing Bear for many years. A contemporary of his son, Brenna's father, Winona had grieved with the family when Brenna's parents had died in one of Absaroka's infrequent cyclonic weather disturbances.

But she had never supported John's unshakable belief that humanity's alien enemy, the Bug-Eyes, would return.

"Sister Standing Bear," Principal Chief Old Coyote said, "will you relinquish the floor?"

Brenna nodded. "I will." She resumed her seat, outwardly calm, but fighting a rising panic. Now she would need every bit of skill she could muster to win the council's approval. This wasn't a new petition. They had heard her grandfather's arguments before. But this time Brenna intended to bring ancient memories to the surface. To remind her people of things her grandfather had been unwilling to voice.

"Thank you, Sister." Winona Old Coyote gazed around the central chamber. "Our sister raises an old argument. John Standing Bear often harangued this council to build a planetary fleet." Nods of agreement and more than a few smiles met her statement.

"The Planetary Council is well aware of Sister Standing Bear's family phobia regarding the Bug-Eyes." She turned to Brenna, her expression sorrowful. "We appreciate your grandfather's military service and sympathize with the horrors he experienced aboard the *Ascension* during the Bug-Eye invasion." She paused, granting time for attention to focus on her words.

"But we are also aware," the principal chief continued, "that there has been no further sign of the Bug-Eyes in the ensuing sixty-eight years. This council has not seen fit to expend the resources or manpower necessary to build and man a fleet against a threat that does not exist ... except in the mind of one elderly warrior, who has now joined his ancestors, and the grandchild he indoctrinated quite thoroughly."

A silence so profound it pressed against Brenna's soul descended on the chamber. She inhaled deeply, marshaled her strength, and stood.

"With your permission, Elder?"

Principal Chief Old Coyote nodded and folded into her seat.

"I believe, as did my grandfather, that the Bug-Eyes will return." She paused while a susurrus of whispers flowed around the room. "I also believe," she continued and the chamber quieted, "that we are foolish to place all our trust in the USL."

Councilman Wolfclaw shot to his feet. "What basis do you have for impugning the USL? Why, your own grandfather served with their fleet. He knew them to be an honorable and trustworthy service. He fought for our inclusion in the Universal Star League, and that membership guarantees that the USL will protect this planet from all enemies."

Brenna's heart raced and she raised sweat-damp palms as if to ward off his words.

"Forgive me, Elder," she said. "I did not mean to imply that the USL was untrustworthy..."

"But you said..."

Winona Old Coyote's gavel sounded, bringing them both to silence. "Sister Standing Bear has the floor, Councilman. Please allow her to finish."

Councilman Wolfclaw scowled, but sat down.

"Thank you, Principal Chief." Clasping her hands to control their shaking, Brenna continued. "I agree that the USL is an honorable service and I am not saying that they would intentionally fail us. However," she turned slightly to include the audience, "can you not imagine a scenario where the USL was so besieged by pleas for help that they could not answer all? Though their flex-drive can bring ships to our aid almost instantly, what would happen if multiple worlds were attacked simultaneously? Would they not be forced to triage?"

Brenna paused while council and listeners alike absorbed her words.

"Absaroka is a small planet. Our population is negligible compared to many of the Universal Star League worlds. If faced with more requests than they could handle, would not the USL fleet go where the greatest numbers were at risk?"

The central chamber was so quiet Brenna could hear her own pulse pounding in her ears. They heard her. She must deliver her final blow before they had time to assemble arguments.

"Also," she said, keeping her voice quiet so that her listeners would need to pay close attention to her words, "there is the matter of history. On Earth, when a purely human enemy invaded our land, our ancestors were unprepared. They failed to acknowledge the threat until it was too late, and so were unable to protect our people. Our nations were nearly exterminated, our cultures almost obliterated."

"Now that we have regained our heritage, now that our nations have chosen to abandon Earth and begin again on Absaroka, let us not repeat the mistakes of our fathers. Let us never again fail to protect our people. Especially not from an alien race that destroyed whole worlds in their last incursion. Absaroka escaped the Bug-Eye's notice sixty-eight years ago. We cannot expect to be so lucky again."

Silence reigned. Brenna completed her argument.

"I believe the Universal Star League is a great system. I believe that the USL will do everything they can to protect

Absaroka in the event of invasion. I also believe that Absaroka has a duty to be prepared to defend herself. We have a proud and noble heritage. Let us honor the warriors of our past by producing a new breed of warrior: the Warbirds of Absaroka."

A war cry sounded from the audience; it rang through the chamber. Brenna turned toward the sound only to be met by an escalation of yips and ululations.

Her soul calmed. Her people had heard her. She was content.

2

*B*renna stood at the viewport, staring intently into the inky blackness of flexed space. Nothing was to be seen while the commercial transport's flex-drive was engaged, but she didn't want to miss the instant of Earth's appearance against the backdrop of infinite space. Her first glimpse of the world that was the Great Mother of all humanity should be a sacred experience.

When the Planetary Council had first charged her with this mission, she had balked.

"Me? Go to Earth and buy a space ship?" she had asked.

"Who else?" Principal Chief Old Coyote had countered. "This is your idea, sister. Your grandfather's dream. You are the perfect choice."

"But I don't know anything about space ships or military tactics," she'd retorted. "I wouldn't know what to look for!"

"Learn," the Principal Chief had commanded.

The ship hummed around her as it prepared to drop out of flex-drive, and Brenna leaned closer to the viewport's transparent surface. With an infinitesimal shudder, the ship dropped into normal space and Earth materialized before Brenna's dazzled eyes. She soaked up the vision of the blue and green globe, of the white clouds that swirled and shifted, shrouding the land masses and oceans alike.

Earth! She was actually staring at the planet that had given birth to them all.

Giddy laughter swelled in her chest, but she contained it, contenting herself with a broad smile. Grandfather had told her so many stories of Earth. She longed to see its majestic mountains, wade in its clear, clean streams, observe its plains teeming with wildlife! In a matter of hours, she, Brenna Standing Bear, would step onto the magical, mystical planet her grandfather had immortalized.

Breathing deeply, Brenna pulled herself from her awed reverie. She wasn't visiting Earth on a spirit quest, she was here on a mission. She had six months to familiarize herself with military history, strategy, and the technical details of the various classes of military space vessels. Before she returned to Absaroka, she intended to purchase the flagship of the fleet they would build.

The enormity of her task overwhelmed her and she breathed a quiet prayer. "Guide me, Grandfather. Don't let me fail our people."

Two hours later, Brenna stepped out of the shuttle and onto Earth. At least, she stepped onto the surface of the commercial transport's shuttle bay in the spaceport at New Atlantis. Far from open sky and grassy plains teeming with animals, she found herself in a multistory building thronged with thousands of people of every race and nationality.

She'd never seen so many people ... or so vast a structure. Why, the crowd flowing around her could very well be equal to the entire population of Absaroka. Everywhere she looked her sight was assaulted by color and movement. The crowd ebbed and flowed like a river swelled by torrential rainfall. Men, women, and children clad in clothing styles she'd never dreamed of — flowing garments that trailed the wearers like wisps of clouds, form-fitting unitards that left nothing to the imagination, headdresses so elaborate Brenna wondered how the wearers maintained their balance. Reds, purples, greens, oranges, colors she had no words to describe. The variety was endless and overwhelming.

Mechanized voices repeated instructions while conversations buzzed in every tone and timbre imaginable. Loud and soft. Brash and soothing. Demanding and whining. If a human voice could produce it, Brenna heard it among the throng that surrounded her.

And the odors! Hot oil and spices from food carts whose vendors shouted the delights of their wares, rich floral perfumes, and the earthy musk of human bodies packed too closely together.

Her head ached from sensory overload. She wanted nothing more than to run back onto the shuttle and demand to be returned to the peace of Absaroka.

"I'm not here for pleasure," she reminded herself grimly. "My comfort is unimportant. I have a job to do. My people are counting on me."

Settling her pack more comfortably on her shoulders, Brenna joined the queue waiting to be processed through customs.

3

$\mathcal{B}$renna leaned back in her chair at the reference library at the USL Academy. The carrel in the back of the military history section had become an office of sorts for her during the last five months. She stood, stretched, and noted with satisfaction that her collection of sim-card note files had grown significantly during her tenure in the library. Few reference sources remained that she hadn't at least skimmed. She was particularly proud of the files she had amassed on military vessels.

She now knew the difference between a battleship, a cruiser, a destroyer, a frigate, and a fighter. She understood which methods of propulsion were used in which circumstances: flex-drive to cover interstellar distances in a matter of hours; conventional thrusters for navigating within a solar system. And the armament necessary for the defense of Absaroka: mag-rail guns, nuclear warheads, gigawatt laser canons fitted to specialized turrets, and the fearsome anti-matter weapons.

Brenna's shopping list was long and she knew it would take years to fill, but she had a plan now, and knew what she hoped to purchase before her return to Absaroka next month.

With a smile of satisfaction, she packed the contents of her cubicle for the last time. Her time of study was at an end. Now was the time for action.

She left the reference library and strode to the main administration building of the USL. The white marble and glass edifice glistened in the afternoon sun. Twenty stories tall, the building's footprint covered more ground than any ten buildings on Absaroka — even the imposing Longhouse. Brenna shook her head. She'd never look at her own world with the same eyes again.

Though she would never admit her feelings to another soul, Brenna was disappointed by Earth. The stories her grandfather had told had led her to believe Earth was a paradise. Its waters purer than anywhere else in the universe, its mountains more glorious, and its plains teeming with wildlife. Reality told an entirely different story. Earth certainly had its merits — gleaming cities, both terrestrial and aquatic, and amazing technological research and development stations — but the land itself, the mystical entity that had always been sacred to her people, had been subsumed by the works of men.

No, Brenna would not long for Earth when she left. She was glad to have had the opportunity to visit, but she was content to live out her life on Absaroka. And she was pleased with the care her people lavished on their new home, and proud that she had convinced its leadership to defend it properly.

With that defense in mind, she strode confidently to the main desk of the administration building.

A young woman with elaborately styled hair and wearing a USL uniform smiled and asked, "May I be of service?"

Brenna straightened her shoulders and assumed her most official expression. "I'm here to buy a battleship. With whom should I speak?"

The young woman's eyes widened and her unnaturally pink

lips formed a small 'O' of surprise before she caught herself and regained her pleasant, but neutral expression. "Forgive me," she said, "but that's an unusual request. If you'll be seated, I'll contact my superior." She motioned Brenna to an alcove of sleek-lined chairs and tables before turning to a display embedded in a console behind her.

Brenna moved to the alcove, seated herself and reviewed her notes on what she hoped to purchase for Absaroka. The Planetary Council had given her a strict budget. A set amount for her personal use during her stay on Earth, food, lodging, transportation, incidentals, and an enormous amount for the purchase of a military vessel and the hiring of a crew to transport the craft to Absaroka. At least, the amount had seemed enormous to everyone on Absaroka. Now that she'd lived on Earth for five months, Brenna could only hope the budget would be sufficient for their needs.

After what seemed like an eternity, a dark-skinned man with graying hair and an impeccably fitted USL uniform approached her. She recognized the insignia of an admiral on his jacket and stood at once.

"My name is Admiral Jacobs," he said, offering her his hand. "and I understand you're interested in purchasing a battleship."

"Yes. Thank you," she said, shaking his proffered hand. "I'm Brenna Standing Bear, a representative of the Confederated Nations of Absaroka. We wish to build a fleet for planetary defense."

Admiral Jacobs motioned to the chairs. "Why don't we sit down and discuss this decision. May I ask why your government wishes to go to the expense of building a fleet? Absaroka is a Universal Star League planet, is it not?"

Brenna steeled herself, bringing the old arguments to mind. "Yes. We are a member of Universal Star League, and we appreciate and honor USL's pledge to defend our world," she paused, glanced at her hands and licked her lips.

"But?" the admiral encouraged.

"Well, you see, sir, my grandfather fought in the Bug-Eye War. He was an engineer assigned to the *USL Ascension*, and he … well, he always felt that the Bug-Eyes would return. That no matter how prepared the USL is, in the case of a catastrophic, coordinated attack, the fleet wouldn't be able to defend everyone." She paused again and then blurted out, "And we're an insignificant planet, with no strategic value."

She raised her eyes and glared at the admiral. "We need to be able to defend ourselves. We *need* a planetary fleet."

Admiral Jacobs nodded, his expression somber. "Your grandfather was a wise man and your government was well-advised to listen to him."

Brenna's jaw dropped. "You're not insulted?" she asked.

He smiled. "Not at all. I only wish more of our member worlds would follow your example." He stood, motioning Brenna to join him. "Let's go to my office and discuss your specific needs and budget. I'm sure we'll be able to work something out."

After discussing terms, Jacobs requested a pilot and shuttle, and took Brenna to the USL supply spaceport where available ships were docked. She was glad of their talk. In addition to the financial negotiation, the admiral had provided invaluable insight into her plans for the fleet.

"I want a battleship as flagship of the fleet," she'd said. "That's what I'm hoping for today. Then, over the next several years, I want to add three destroyers, five cruisers, and at least six fighters."

He had nodded. "That's a good start. But even for a planet of your modest size, I'd recommend at least five destroyers and ten cruisers, twelve if you can swing it. And as for the fighters, you'll want a minimum of three squads, with five fighters in each."

Her eyes had widened. "That's fifteen fighters," she'd whispered. "Over twice what I was dreaming of."

"I know," he said. "You'll have your work cut out for you back home, but if the need ever arises, you'll be glad of the extra birds."

Reviewing that conversation now, Brenna smiled. Birds. Yes. If … no, *when* she got them, she'd see that the fighters were named after birds of prey.

"Coming up on the spaceport now, Admiral," the pilot said, breaking into Brenna's thoughts. "Do you want me to dock?"

"No, take us on a fly-by of the new *smart-steel* battleships. We'll dock with the *Sequoia* when we're finished."

Jacobs turned to Brenna. "I know you don't have the budget for one of these new ships, but I want you to see what we'll be able to bring to your defense." He smiled tightly. "Hopefully this will be the only time you'll ever see them."

Brenna marveled at the sleek, deadly looking battleships as Jacobs explained the new technology. "The hull plating is comprised of a technologically advanced substance our engineers have dubbed *vari-steel*. It's a newly created semi-metal, designed to be incredibly dense and difficult to penetrate, but without the weight or thickness of traditional tungsten plating."

After docking with the *Sequoia*, Jacobs gave her a tour of the old-style battleship. While not as sleek and shiny as the vari-steel ships, the *Sequoia* appeared to be in good order. Any scars she might have incurred in battle had been lovingly repaired and burnished over.

"She's not new," Jacobs said, guiding Brenna onto the bridge, "but she's in good running order. All her systems have been overhauled and she's ready for deep space."

Brenna nodded, walking the circumference of the bridge,

running fingers over control panels and noting the odor of cleaning solvents mixed with fresh oil. Every surface fairly glistened with cleanliness.

"She's Ascension-class, isn't she?" Brenna asked. When the admiral agreed, she said, "How old?"

"She was commissioned at the end of the Bug-Eye War, so roughly sixty-eight years old."

Brenna made her decision. She slapped her hand on the back of the captain's chair, feeling the give of the supple leather. "We'll take her. Now, what can we do about a crew to transport her to Absaroka? And we'll need competent instructors to train our own crews, and to advise us on future purchases as we grow our fleet."

Admiral Jacobs held out his hand and Brenna shook it firmly. He laid his other hand atop their clasped ones. "You've made a good choice. She'll serve you well. Let's return to headquarters and we'll work out a plan for crew and instructors."

"One more thing," she said as they left the bridge, "will we be able to rename her?"

"Of course. I'll see that you have the necessary forms to take back to your planetary government."

4

Warchief Brenna Standing Bear studied the cloud-enshrouded green and blue marble that was her home world, Absaroka. From the viewscreen in her ready room she enjoyed the never-ending swirl of cloud formations across the planet's face as weather patterns built, shifted and broke apart. The Confederated Nations had done well when they chose this planet. Absaroka was not Earth, would never be Earth, but it had mountains and forests, clear blue lakes and rivers, and large continental masses sprinkled among its oceans. And the face it showed to its children orbiting in space was unendingly beautiful.

The seven years since her grandfather's death and her successes with the Planetary Council and the USL Academy had changed Brenna. She was no longer a simple citizen of Absaroka. The principal chief had decided that since she had fought for and hand-picked most of the fleet, she should be prepared to lead it.

Since the purchase of *USL Sequoia*, which the people of Absaroka had re-christened *CNS Thunderbird*, the Planetary Council had rounded out Absaroka's fleet with five destroyers (named for the original Five Civilized Tribes – *CNS Choctaw*, *Chickasaw*, *Creek*, *Seminole*, and *Cherokee*), twelve cruisers (each named for another of the tribes of the Confederated Nations), and fifteen warbirds — fighters in the USL parlance. Each warbird had been named by its pilot for an old Earth bird of prey.

Brenna smiled. Her warriors might be untested in battle, but Absaroka's fleet was well-trained and ready to defend its home world. She prayed that she and her grandfather had been wrong, that the Bug-Eyes would never return and her fleet would never need to do more than keep Absaroka free of criminal factions.

A single bell-like tone broke her reverie. Brenna turned from the splendor of Absaroka to a flashing light on her comm unit. Acknowledging the signal, she asked, "Yes, Mister Sparrow Hawk?"

"Warchief, the fleet awaits your command to begin the readiness exercise."

"Very well. Chief Whitehorse is authorized to assume command. The action will commence at his pleasure; obey him well. Warchief Standing Bear out."

"Understood, Warchief. It shall be done."

The comm unit deactivated and Brenna turned back to her viewscreen. Settling deeper into her command chair, she focused the screen on her fleet. Alex Whitehorse would command the exercise from the fleet command bridge here on their flagship, *CNS Thunderbird*. Alex was a good officer and commanded his destroyer, *CNS Cherokee*, efficiently and effectively, but he lacked experience leading more than a single ship. This exercise would test his ability to see beyond his own ship's maneuverability. Determine if he had what it took to direct a fleet.

Brenna would watch the action from the comfort of her

ready room behind *Thunderbird's* main bridge. She would not interfere with her subordinate's decisions, but she would weigh them against her own instincts as well as analyze their outcome. She needed a second in command, and the chiefs of her five destroyers were all being scrutinized to determine their fitness. Each was a fine ship's commander, but it took more than the ability to lead a single crew to make a warchief, and Brenna's second in command would be in line to be her successor.

The war exercise commenced and Brenna watched with interest as her fleet ran through their paces.

5

Chief Alex Whitehorse watched his fleet deploy across the multiple screens of the warchief's console in fleet command, a secondary bridge in a remote and well-protected section of *Thunderbird's* interior. His thought flickered to Warchief Standing Bear, who normally occupied this seat, wondering how she felt about giving him command. He pushed the thought aside as irrelevant. This exercise was as much about training him as it was the fleet. Warchief Standing Bear needed a second in command. This was his chance to show her that he was up to the task.

Alex opened a direct line to his own second, Randy Foxfire, who occupied the captain's chair on *Cherokee's* bridge while Alex commanded the fleet. "Commander Foxfire, report."

"All is in readiness, Chief," Randy said, his tone clear and confident. "We're standing by."

"Acknowledged." Alex opened a line to *Thunderbird's* XO. "Mister Blackcloud, report."

"The first squad of warbirds is ready to launch, Chief," the XO said. "Second squad is standing by."

"Understood." Alex toggled the line to the destroyer *Choctaw*. "Chief Littlebear, begin evasive maneuvers."

"Yes sir," said Amanda Littlebear's calm voice.

Alex switched back to *Thunderbird's* bridge. "Mister Blackcloud, *Choctaw* is your target. Get your birds in flight."

"Acknowledged, sir."

Alex settled back to watch the imitation dance of death. This was simply a training exercise, everyone involved was part of his team, but the purpose was deadly serious. With loaded and unguarded weapons, this dance could turn fatal.

He knew that too many of the young warbird pilots considered this no more than a real-life version of a holostar. A game that aroused the senses and sent adrenaline flowing through their veins. While he prayed that their perception would never need to change, he pushed their training so that their reactions would become instinctual. Muscle memory could save their lives if a real attack ever came.

The *Choctaw*, with warbirds in pursuit, danced around Absaroka's orbit as though its movements had been choreographed. The squads of warbirds flitted in and out of *Thunderbird's* flight decks like hummingbirds, landing, refueling, and darting back into the imagined fray with seeming effortlessness.

All but one.

Alex straightened in his chair, ready to open a line to the Chief of the Deck, when he saw the man signal the pilot out of *Falcon*. Opening his receiver, he listened in on the confrontation.

"Just what do you think you're doing out there, Pilot Leaping Trout?" the COD growled.

"Followin' orders, shir," Caleb Leaping Trout answered with a distinct slur to his words.

"I don't think so, mister," barked the COD. "You've been sluggish answering your hails and sloppy with the formations." He stopped, leaned toward the young man and then backed away quickly. "And you stink of whiskey. That's it. You're grounded, and confined to quarters until Chief Whitehorse has time to deal with you. Dismissed."

"Bu...but..." Caleb sputtered.

"I said, 'Dismissed,' Pilot Leaping Trout. Do you need me to draw you a picture?" The COD leaned close and glared at the younger man.

"No sir ... I mean, yes sir," he said, confused. Not sure what response was required, he stumbled away from the COD and off the flight deck.

The COD waved one of his men over. "Follow Caleb," he said. "Make sure he gets to his quarters and then stand guard until you're relieved."

"Yes sir," he said, saluting and then turning on his heel to follow the impaired pilot.

Alex closed the receiver and turned his attention back to his screens. Too bad. Caleb Leaping Trout had been a promising pilot, but years with the fleet had taught him that early promise was not always realized. He'd have to reward the COD's astute observation and quick action. An impaired pilot was a danger to his entire squad.

The rest of the exercise went flawlessly. Alex moved the fleet's ships into standard formations, textbook patterns that any chief would recognize, then, with his next set of orders, produced a variation of his own devising. Whatever he ordered, his fleet carried out his commands with precision.

He smiled. No one questioned his orders, even on the most obscure formation. His people trusted him. A wave of gratitude washed over him. He'd do everything in his power to be worthy of that trust.

6

*B*renna was impressed. No matter what Chief Whitehorse ordered, and some of those formations were completely unorthodox, the fleet obeyed with alacrity. She nodded. Yes. Alex Whitehorse would make a fine second.

She stretched out her hand to hail Alex, wanting to congratulate him on an exemplary exercise, when alarms blared and lights flashed throughout the ship. She whirled to her monitor to discover the source of the problem, and found it immediately. An unknown vessel had materialized just beyond Absaroka's orbit.

"Warchief Standing Bear," Alex's voice sounded through Brenna's comm unit. "An unknown ship is in our space; they're not answering our hails. Do you wish to take command of the fleet?"

Brenna frowned. She'd pushed to standing the instant the vessel appeared on her screens. Her fingers itched for the controls of her chair on the fleet command bridge, but she knew better than to change horses in mid-stream.

"No, Chief Whitehorse. The fleet is responding well to your commands. A change now would disrupt that flow. We need everyone at their best. Carry on. I'll observe and advise from here."

"I hear and obey, Warchief."

Before either of them could react, the strange vessel glowed green and then aimed a fine energy stream at the *Choctaw*. The destroyer imploded. One moment Chief Amanda Littlebear's vessel held its place in the latest formation, and the next it was extinguished in a blinding flare of light.

"Chief Whitehorse," Brenna yelled into the comm unit, "what just happened?"

"My officers are reporting now, Warchief."

As Brenna waited she noted fighters emerging from the enemy carrier. Alex Whitehorse ordered the warbirds out to meet them. Fourteen small, sleek birds of prey launched and zipped around the enemy fighters. Lasers streaked red and blue against interstellar black.

"Warchief, all our readings suggest a singularity event took out the *Choctaw*, and that carrier and its fighters ... their patterns are reading as Bug-Eye vessels." Alex paused for only a fraction of a second. "You were right, Brenna. They've returned."

Brenna slumped back into her chair, then pounded the armrest. "I never believed we had truly defeated them," she said quietly, "but I always hoped." She straightened her spine and narrowed her eyes. "Carry on, Chief Whitehorse. You're in command. This is what we've trained for. This is why our fleet exists. Protect our people."

"Yes, Warchief. It has been my honor to serve with you."

"And mine as well, Alex. May the Great Spirit guide you."

Thunderbird's XO took his orders from Alex, as Brenna had ordered, but Brenna commandeered one of the flagship's top communications officers to assist her in her ready room. Messages flashed between the *Thunderbird* and the Longhouse as Brenna apprised the leaders of her people of their imminent danger.

[Flagship to Planetary Council]: We are under attack. This is not an exercise. Repeat. This is not an exercise.

[Planetary Council to Flagship]: We see the ship, but do not recognize its configuration. Have you identified?

[Flagship to Planetary Council]: Identification confirmed: Bug-Eye. Notify USL via flex-space communication. *Choctaw* destroyed. All ships engaged. New weapon in play. May threaten whole planet if we fail.

[Planetary Council to Flagship]: Message received and relayed to USL. Godspeed, Warchief. May the Great Spirit guide you. Absaroka out.

Absaroka didn't have the resources to evacuate the planet, and Brenna was all too aware that with a singularity weapon, her fleet was the only thing standing between the Confederated Nations and annihilation.

Even if the tribes could have escaped the planet, they had no idea how many Bug-Eye ships waited just beyond Absaroka's orbit.

Principal Chief Old Coyote had sent the distress call to USL command. Brenna and the fleet had to hold the enemy at bay long enough for their allies to arrive.

Assuming other Universal Star League worlds weren't under attack as well.

Great Spirit! Brenna wished that her long ago arguments had remained hypothetical.

She paced her ready room listening to the shouted messages from *Cherokee* and the other destroyers and cruisers, and watching the decimation of her fleet on the viewscreen. She'd now seen two of her destroyers (*Choctaw* and *Seminole*) and three of her cruisers (*Kiowa*, *Lakota*, and *Ute*) implode. Each time the Swarm carrier hung motionless against the backdrop of space while the deadly green glow built, and each time the fine energy stream touched one of her ships, it disappeared in a blinding flash.

She had to do something. She couldn't just pace this room and wait for *Thunderbird* to implode. Forcing herself to calm, Brenna watched a replay of the destruction of the *Kiowa*. The enemy vessel hung motionless while the green glow built. The enemy fighters were particularly active during the waiting period. Almost ...

Could that be a flaw?

Could the ship be vulnerable while it charged?

What if...?

But no, her fourteen warbirds were already down to nine, they couldn't afford to waste one on an untested theory. But if it were true? Could they afford *not* to try?

Her thoughts circled like birds of prey over a dying animal. She was missing something. Something important. And then the necessary datum clicked into place.

Fourteen. There had been *fourteen* warbirds in the fray. Now there were nine.

Brenna raced from the ready room into her private quarters, stripping as she ran. Without giving herself time to think about consequences or unrealized futures or things left undone, she grabbed her flight suit and pulled it on. She wasn't the pilot those youngsters were, but she could fly and the mission she had in mind didn't require finesse.

Grabbing her helmet she made a mad dash to the flight deck, screaming orders over her wrist comm to the COD as she ran. "Get the *Falcon* ready," she yelled. "I'm going out!"

"But Warchief," the COD cried, "you can't."

"I can and I will, Chief," she answered. "Obey my command."

"Yes, Warchief," the man said crisply.

Panting, Brenna hurtled onto the flight deck, paused to catch her breath, and secured her helmet to the neck of her flight suit. Crew members finished positioning the *Falcon* for take off as Brenna moved forward.

The Chief of the Deck stepped in front of her and saluted. "Warchief Standing Bear, may I ask for your flight plan?"

She gave the man a crooked smile, returned his salute, and shook her helmeted head. "You may not, Chief," she replied. "You may, however, give my regards and utmost thanks to Chief Whitehorse. You stand as witness that he is my designated choice to replace me as Warchief, should any of us survive. Thank you for your service, Chief. It has been an honor to serve our people with you."

The COD's jaw clenched. He nodded and stood at attention as Brenna climbed into the *Falcon*. She jumped the compact little warbird into the void as soon as she was strapped in.

"Pilot Standing Bear, just what the hell do you think you're doing?" Alex Whitehorse's voice was loud and commanding in her ear.

"What happened to the deference due a warchief?" she asked.

"It went out the window when she stopped acting like one," he snapped. "I repeat, what the hell do you think you're doing, Brenna?"

"Something I will not order one of my pilot's to do," she gathered her thoughts for a moment before deciding. The warchief needed as much information as possible. "Listen, Alex," she said overriding him as he started to object. "I have a theory that the Bug-Eye ship may be vulnerable as that green charge builds. I won't risk one of our pilots to test this, but I'm willing to do it myself."

She took a shuddering breath, waiting for a response that didn't come. Really, what could Alex say?

"The fleet is yours, Alex. If this works, I'll buy you some time and provide some much-needed information. If it doesn't, guard Absaroka as best you can until the USL fleet arrives." She snapped off her communications before he could respond. Sometimes, it was good to be alone with one's own thoughts.

You were right, Grandfather, she thought. *The Bug-Eyes have returned. I built the fleet as you wanted, but it wasn't enough.*

She positioned the *Falcon* where she could observe the carrier, trusting Alex to ensure that the other warbirds kept the Bug-Eye's fighters off her tail. She watched the deadly dance of the birds of prey while she waited. At last the carrier paused in its restless movement and the green glow began to build.

Brenna inhaled deeply, pushed the *Falcon* to ramming speed, and thought with love of the blue-green marble that twirled in the atmosphere below. She was proud to have been warchief of her people, proud to have been tasked with the defense of Absaroka. Her grandfather had entrusted this legacy to her, and she had not failed him.

Brenna Standing Bear rammed the Bug-Eye carrier as it hung motionless in space, and imploded with her enemy in a singularity of purpose.

COPYRIGHT

ALSO BY DEB LOGAN

Children's Stories and Chapter Books:

Cinnamon Chou Files:

- THE CASE OF THE MISSING INARIAN
- THE CASE OF THE GLITTERING HOARD
- THE CASE OF THE RECREATIONAL THIEF
- THE CASE OF THE VANISHING PUPPY

Prentiss Twins Novels:

- THUNDERBIRD
- COYOTE
- WHITE BUFFALO (COMING SOON!)
- THE TWELVE DAYS OF TRICKSTERS (A PRENTISS TWINS SHORT STORY)

"Read-to-Me" Stories:

- CHATTERMASTER
- DEIRDRE'S DRAGON
- THE FOX AND THE FLEAS
- MOM'S HELPER
- READ-TO-ME STORIES (COLLECTION)

Short Stories:

- ANGELIC VOICES
- LILAH'S GHOST

Young Adult Stories and Novels:

Dani Erickson Stories:

- DEMON DAZE
- SCHOOL DAZE
- FAMILY DAZE
- CHALLENGING DAZE
- DANGEROUS DAZE
- DANI'S DEMONS (COLLECTION)

Faery Chronicles:

- FAERY UNEXPECTED (NOVEL)
- FAERY BEAUTIFUL (SHORT STORY)
- FAERY UNPREDICTABLE (NOVELETTE)
- LEXIE'S CHOICE (SHORT STORY)
- OF DRAGONS AND CENTAURS (SHORT STORY)
- FAERY COLLECTIBLE (COLLECTION)

Feyland Tie-Ins:

- EMMA: A FEYLAND DRYAD
- ON GUARD: A FEYLAND STORY

Seer Chronicles:

- TERRORS
- TO HAVE...AND TO HOLD
- SELKIES IN PARADISE
- THE JOURNAL
- PALADIN SHIELD

Siren Tales:

- Salt Water
- Siren Surf

Short Story Collections:

- Ghosts and Ghoulies
- More Ghosts and Ghoulies

Short Fiction:

- Amelia Fox: Spy in Training
- Beauty or Butterface?
- Rush!
- That Lake House Summer

"WDM Presents" Anthologies:

- Tales of Mystery & Mayhem
- 2016: A Year of Short Fiction
- 2017: A Year of Short Fiction
- WDM Presents: Short Fiction from 2019
- WDM Presents: Short Fiction from 2020

ABOUT DEB LOGAN

Deb Logan specializes in tales for the young – and the young at heart! Author of the popular Faery Chronicles series, Deb loves the unknown, whether it's the lure of space or earthbound mythology. She writes about demon hunters, thunderbirds, and everyday life on a space station for tweens, teens, and anyone who enjoys young adult fiction. Her work has been published in multiple volumes of *Fiction River*, as well as in *2017 Young Explorer's Adventure Guide*, F*eyland Tales*, and other popular anthologies.

Sign up for Deb's newsletter and receive a FREE story!

To learn more, visit Deb at:
debloganwrites.com
Or send her an email at:
debloganwrites@gmail.com

ALSO BY DEBBIE MUMFORD

Kristi Lundrigan Mysteries:

- DELECTABLE MOUNTAIN QUILTING (NOVEL)
- FOOL'S PUZZLE (SHORT STORY)
- WILDFIRE! (SHORT STORY)

Gus and Ghost Short Story Series:

- SEVENTH
- SEVENTH: FIRST FRUITS
- DEATH OF AN ALCHEMIST (UNCOLLECTED ANTHOLOGY)
- SEVENTH: THE SAMHAIN DILEMMA

Logans of Lastalrig Series:

- HER HIGHLAND LAIRD (NOVELLA)
- HER HIGHLAND YULE (SHORT STORY)

Red's Series:

- RED'S MAGICK (SHORT STORY COLLECTION)
- SEEING RED (SHORT STORY)

Signs of the Prophecy Novels:

- YOUNGEST
- SEEKER
- CHOSEN (COMING SOON!)

Sorcha's Children Series:

- SORCHA'S CHILDREN (OMNIBUS EDITION)
- SORCHA'S HEART (NOVELLA)
- DRAGONS' CHOICE (NOVEL)
- DRAGONS' FLIGHT (NOVEL)
- DRAGONS' DESIRE (NOVEL)
- DRAGONS' DESTINY (NOVEL)

Supernatural Yellowstone Short Story Series:

- REALITY BITES
- THE CAT LADY OF YELLOWSTONE

Uncollected Anthology Short Stories:

- DEATH OF AN ALCHEMIST (UA ALCHEMY)
- THE WEDDING CAKE (UA MAGICAL ARTS)

Universal Star League Short Story Series:

- THE WARBIRDS OF ABSAROKA
- AWAKENING THE WARRIOR
- INCIDENT ON THE ODYSSEY
- THE QUEEN'S CAPTIVE
- THE LOST COLONY
- VOYAGES INTO THE BLACK (COLLECTION)

Witchling Short Story Series:

- WITCHLING
- THE SOLITARY SORCERESS
- TO PROTECT A PRINCESS

Stand Alone Novels:

- Second Sight

Short Story Collections:

- Love in a Flash
- Tales of Bygone Days
- Tales of Love & Magick
- Tales of the Unexpected
- Tales of Tomorrow
- Tales of Disastrous Deeds

Short Fiction:

- A Walk with Georgia
- Astromancer
- Beneath and Beyond
- Deep Dreaming
- Delia's Decision
- Ice Storm
- Incident on the High Line
- Miss Bainbridge's Summer Adventure
- Needle-Green
- New Year
- Opening Her Eyes
- Remembrance
- Silver-Tipped Death
- Sisters in Suffrage
- Skye Dreams
- Spinning
- The Tie That Binds
- The Trail Where We Cried

- THE WHITE DRAGON AND THE RED
- TO DREAM OF FLYING
- TREASURES
- WAKINYAN'S VALLEY

"WDM Presents" Anthologies:

- TALES OF MYSTERY & MAYHEM
- 2016: A YEAR OF SHORT FICTION
- 2017: A YEAR OF SHORT FICTION
- WDM PRESENTS: SHORT FICTION FROM 2019
- WDM PRESENTS: SHORT FICTION FROM 2020

ABOUT DEBBIE MUMFORD

Debbie Mumford specializes in speculative fiction (fantasy, paranormal romance, and science fiction) as well as mystery and historical fiction. Author of the popular *Sorcha's Children* series, Debbie loves the unknown, whether it's the lure of space or earthbound mythology. Her work has been published in multiple volumes of *Fiction River*, as well as in *Heart's Kiss Magazine*, *Amazing Monster Tales*, and many other popular anthologies. She writes about dragon-shifters, time-traveling lovers, and detectives—whether amateur or professional.

Join Debbie's special announcement newsletter list and receive a FREE story!

To learn more, visit Debbie at:
debbiemumford.com/
Or send her an email at:
deborah.mumford@gmail.com

facebook.com/DebbieMumfordWrites
amazon.com/author/debbiemumford
bookbub.com/authors/debbie-mumford
twitter.com/deborah_mumford

COPYRIGHT